PRAISE FOR *THE STRANGER GAME*

'An enigmatic novel . . . a metaphysical thriller'
Edmund White

'Like the best of Highsmith and Hitchcock rolled into one'
Marisa Silver

'Beautiful, thoughtful meditation on the invisible
ties that bind us–even to strangers'
Kirkus Reviews

'Engrossing.... Those with a taste for the offbeat
will find this well worth reading'
Publishers Weekly

'A phenomenal mystery novel filled with action and a story
line that makes you think about human interaction'
The Oklahoman

'This is Patricia Highsmith-style suspense, edgy and a little
dreamy, with a sense of uncertainty lurking everywhere'
Booklist

'A fun, moody, twisty thriller, with a sun-touched, West
Coast vibe...as much Joan Didion as Patricia Highsmith'
Scott Smith

'"Following" gets a whole new meaning in
Peter Gadol's stylish psychological thriller'
Janet Fitch

Peter Gadol is the author of seven novels including *The Stranger Game*, *Silver Lake*, *Light at Dusk*, and *The Long Rain*. His work his been translated for foreign editions and appeared in literary journals, including StoryQuarterly, the Los Angeles Review of Books Quarterly Journal, and Tin House. Gadol lives in Los Angeles, where he is Chair and Professor of the MFA Writing program at Otis College of Art and Design.

Also by Peter Gadol

Coyote
The Mystery Roast
Closer to the Sun
The Long Rain
Light at Dusk
Silver Lake

The Stranger Game

Peter Gadol

ONE PLACE. MANY STORIES

HQ
An imprint of HarperCollins*Publishers* Ltd
1 London Bridge Street
London SE1 9GF

This edition 2019

1
First published in Great Britain by
HQ, an imprint of HarperCollins*Publishers* Ltd 2019

Copyright © Peter Gadol 2019

Peter Gadol asserts the moral right to be
identified as the author of this work.
A catalogue record for this book is
available from the British Library.

ISBN: 9781848457690

MIX
Paper from
responsible sources
FSC www.fsc.org **FSC® C007454**

This book is produced from independently certified FSC™ paper
to ensure responsible forest management.

Printed and bound by CPI Group (UK) Ltd, Croydon CR0 4YY

For Chris
Somehow never strangers

The Stranger Game

1

THE FIRST TIME I FOLLOWED ANYONE WAS ON A SUN-
day afternoon in late November, the sky still gray with
ash some weeks after a wildfire to the north. I had gone
out on a hike, hoping to clear my mind by scrambling
up the narrow path of a dry canyon, which worked until
I walked the down trail back to my car. As I was driving
out of the park, I passed a picnic area where there was a
party underway, a birthday celebration with a hacked-at
piñata twirling off a low branch, smoke rising from black-
ened grills, balloons tethered to the benches. At the pe-
riphery, I noticed a little boy, himself a balloon in a red,
round jacket and red, round pants. He didn't seem to be
the center of attention, so I didn't think he was the birthday boy. He must have been about three. He was tossing
an inflated ball, also red, back and forth to his parents,
or not exactly to his parents. He launched the ball instead toward the road where I'd pulled over and parked.

I hadn't planned any of this, but then that was how the game was played, how it began, the first rule: choose your subjects at random.

The balloon boy picked up the ball and tried throwing it again, but he couldn't seem to get it to either parent; it kept falling short. Why didn't they stand closer? Why were they making it difficult for him, was this some kind of test? The boy began flapping his arms, exasperated, until mercifully his mother pulled him aside for a hot dog. The boy's father accepted a beer from another man. Trying to persuade the boy to eat was apparently the wrong move because he shook his head from side to side, cranky right when the afternoon sun both cracked the clouds and began to fade.

The boy's mother scooped him up in her arms, although it looked like he was getting heavy for her, and carried him to a bright green box of a car parked three spaces in front of mine. Did she notice me? No, why would she? There was nothing so peculiar about a forty-year-old woman sitting alone in a gray car idling in a city park. Although that afternoon I was full of longing, and who really knew what I was capable of doing.

The mother fit her boy into a car seat, strapped him in, and brushed his hair off his face. The boy's father had followed them to the car but didn't get in. The woman turned toward him to give him a quick, meaningful kiss, and I heard the man shout as he walked away that he'd call her later when he got home, which elicited an easy smile from the woman.

I revised my story. She was a single mother, right now only dating this man; she'd brought her son to a party the man had said the boy might enjoy. The woman and the man had been seeing each other for six months, and he was the first guy in a long while who she felt was good with her son, better than the boy's actual father. I should have been rooting for them, for their happiness, but I wondered: If the woman and man wound up together permanently, would he be one of those guys who believed their marriage wouldn't be complete until she gave him a child of his own? How would the woman's son handle it? Would the challenge of a new sibling prepare him for all of the other uncertainties ahead, his body changing, the girls or the boys he'd want to take to his own picnics, the inevitable dramas of his own making? Would he continue wearing red jackets with red pants? Would he come into his body as an athlete, or would he excel at piano or math or debate, or all of the above— no, something else, but what?

These were the questions I was asking while trailing the green car out of the park and east along the boulevard, then south, skirting downtown. Traffic gave me cover, but it also meant I had to drive aggressively if I didn't want to lose them. There was an unexpected pleasure in trying to remain unobserved while in pursuit.

Twenty minutes later, we ended up on the east side

of the river heading into a part of the city I didn't know well, and as traffic thinned, it had to be obvious I was behind them. Did the woman see me in her mirror? Did she call her boyfriend and chatter for the sake of it, keeping him on the line in case she needed to tell him a woman wearing dark glasses was following her home?

We were coasting through a newer development, the streets as flat as their map. When the woman turned into a driveway, I continued on and pulled over at the end of the block, five houses away. Now I watched them in my side-view mirror: the woman helped the boy out of the back seat, and she was trying to gather their things and order him into the house, but he was having none of it, sprinting across the yard toward its one leafless tree. Then the boy tripped. He fell first on his knees, then his palms. He wailed.

The woman jogged over and knelt down next to him, righting him, shaking her head, neither angry nor concerned. It wasn't a bad fall. She reached her arms around him and once again she brushed his bangs across his forehead. The boy probably had learned that the longer he wept, the longer his mother would hold him, and so he kept crying. His mother rocked him—and was she smiling? How long would she be able to comfort him like this, her silly boy? I wondered what it was like to be needed in this way, and to know it was a fleeting dependence. The autumn sky turned amber with the last trace of light.

Suddenly from the open back door of the woman's car, the red ball fell out. It rolled all the way down the driveway to the street. Neither the woman nor her son appeared to notice. The breeze carried the ball down the grade toward where I was parked. My first instinct was to hop out and retrieve it and bring it back to the boy, but then I would have revealed my position and possibly alarmed the woman if she put together how far I'd followed her. Also I would have broken the second rule of the game: no contact.

The red ball continued to roll down the middle of the street, pushed on by the evening wind. Would the boy ever find it? Would his mother notice it missing? Was it lost for good? I would never know. I would never see them again. The third rule of the game was never follow the same stranger twice, and so I drove away.

I PREFERRED TO BE IN MY SMALL TIDY HOUSE AT NIGHT rather than during the day because after dark I was less apt to notice whatever I might have been neglecting, the settlement cracks along the ceiling edge or the chipped bathroom tile. No matter the hour though, there was no avoiding the long wardrobe closet I could never fill on my own or the open corner of the main room once occupied by a plain birch writing desk. Then there was the garden all around the lot that existed in a state of permanent disgrace. My ex-boyfriend had been the one who tended to the knotty fall of chaparral down the back slope, although when Ezra moved out, he promised he would come by and take care of this plus the dozen succulents he'd potted during a period of unemployment; he did at first, but then stopped. I noted in my datebook to drench everything every five days. I'd probably over-watered the poor things until they gave up on me. I'd never wanted to own a house by myself, let alone tend its garden. That wasn't the plan. I'd bought the house with marriage in mind. Here was the kitchen where we improvised spice blends, our mortar and pestle verdantly stained; here was the couch where we read aloud to each other the thrillers neither one of us read on our own; here was our bed, our weekend-morning island exile.

I was in a strange mood when I got back from following the woman and her son. I took a bottle of wine out back. High up on the hillside looking west, the city lights looked like an unstrung necklace, the basin covered with bright scattered beads. I kept picturing the way the little boy leaned into his mother, crying, comforted. I thought of myself as someone who would have the capacity to be a good parent to a happy-go-lucky kid, and there was a time when Ezra and I talked about getting pregnant or more likely adoption. Adoption wasn't something I saw myself doing alone; friends did it solo, admirably and well, but that wasn't for me.

I drank the wine fast and poured myself another glass. As I understood it, playing the stranger game was supposed to help you connect (or reconnect) in the most essential way with your fellow beings on the planet, help you renew your sense of empathy, yet I was only left lonelier that night. We were living in dark times, season after season of political uncertainty and social unrest; solitude only amplified my anxiety about the future. Ezra used to have a way of calming me down, and when I was

with him (and when he was in one of his loftier moods),
I believed progress was still possible, that together we
(he and I, all of us) would prevail against the forces that
would undo what we believed in. But Ezra was gone.
He'd disappeared two months earlier. I missed him even
more than I did after the final time we broke up.

A brief history: We had been friendly in college and
shared meals but never dated. We took an art history survey together and then another course on modern move-
ments, and I probably resented the way everything came
to him so effortlessly, good grades, girls smarter than
him. I didn't take him seriously. Two summers after
graduation we re-met at a rooftop party. I was in graduate school and Ezra was copyediting at a magazine. We
stood off in a corner and made up stories about the guests
we didn't know. And we always did that, I have to say,
long before it became part of any faddish game, which
was hardly original, which was something people have
always done while loitering in cafés and airport lounges
or riding trains. Ezra and I were the same height, both
short, which made whispering in each other's ears easy.
Right away I knew I'd always crave his breath against
my neck. Unlike the men I'd been with before, he didn't
become some other animal when we made love later that
night. He was playful, open, but also it was clear he had
his secrets, fish sleeping beneath the surface of a frozen
lake. Unlike the men I'd been with before, he wasn't so

easy to figure out, and I will admit that was what initially drew me to him.

We started taking road trips up the coast. We were curious about the same things, figurative painting, slow-cooked food, small towns far from other small towns. And yet we were also very different people. Ezra often wanted to be alone; I never did. His long black hair had a way of hiding half his glance; I usually pulled mine back into a ponytail. When he didn't shave for a week, it seemed like he was hiding something. I'm grasping for some way to describe what I later understood better from a distance, and I'm dwelling too much on his appearance, although I was very attracted to him and wanted nothing more than to be close to him. His weeklong scruff was soft to touch.

That first morning after the rooftop party, we lay in bed with the blankets thrown back because the radiator was too aggressive. We had nowhere to be. We had all the time in the world for each other. When I was growing up, my father with his aches and pains often told me to enjoy my good health while it lasted and not take it for granted, but maybe the thing we really take for granted in our youth is time: back then an hour lasted longer, each day was epic.

We dated for a couple years and talked about moving in together but never did. Then there was a problem with my lease, I was going to have to move, and I pushed the subject, but Ezra said us sharing an apartment would never work. Never? I asked. As in never ever? My degree was in architecture, and all the way across the country there was a position at a firm that specialized in transforming old factories and warehouses into magnet schools and cultural centers, exactly the kind of work I most wanted to do. When I told Ezra about the job, he said I should go for it if I really wanted to, but he wouldn't follow me out. His declaration came without elaboration and astonished me. We had a bitter fight; he accused me of plotting a course for myself while assuming he'd just fall in, independent Ezra who was sensitive about not getting anywhere in a career of his own. I think I was hurt to the extent I was because his accusation rang true. I applied for the job and got it.

After I moved, Ezra and I stayed in touch; we talked every couple of weeks, and one day my phone trilled with a text. Ezra had come west. He was near my office; in fact, he was at the museum down the street. More specifically, he was in the room with *Madame B in Her Library*, which he knew was my favorite painting, a tall early-modern portrait of a woman confined in a black buttoned-up gown yet grinning at the viewer with conspiratorial bemusement. The library was apparently invisible; the woman was painted against a brown backdrop with no books in sight. I didn't believe Ezra was there. He texted back that there was only one way to find out.

He didn't let go when he hugged me. His narrow shoulders, his veiny arms. His soft beard.

"Oh, Rebecca," he said. "The biggest mistake of my thirty years was not following you out here."

"We're only twenty-eight," I said.

"Whatever. I'm here now."

"What makes you think I'd want you back?" I asked. "How do you know I'm not seeing someone?"

"You're not."

"You don't know that. I don't tell you everything."

"You're not," he said again. "You can't be."

His breath warming my neck.

We lived together for eight years, at some point moving in to the house on the hill, using money my grandmother left me for a down payment. Those first two or three years in that house were the happiest of my life, a paradise to which I would struggle to return. Our last two years together, we argued frequently. I'd left my original job to form a studio with three partners, and we became busy entering every competition we could. We often worked late and through the weekend. Meanwhile Ezra wasn't busy at all; he was always home waiting for me.

I kept up a stupid prolonged flirtation with one of my partners, who was married, which I am pretty sure Ezra never knew about while it was happening. My partner and I never had an actual tryst, and things cooled off, but my infatuation distracted me. The last year with Ezra was terrible. He kept saying he didn't have a place in my life; he was a visitor. I'd tell him he *was* my life, but that sounded thin. I don't have a place in my own life, he'd say, I'm a visitor there, too. I'd say that I didn't know how to respond to that (or what he meant), and he'd snap: Why do you think you have to say anything? Some version of this conversation kept recurring. Then he'd say, I never wanted this house, it's too much. I never wanted this garden, he'd say, or this view, and I'd say, You know that's not true. You're the one who always looked at the listings first. We weren't making love. First tenderness left, then joy. When I got to my studio in the morning, I'd stretch out on a couch for a half hour with my eyes closed until I felt a yoke loosen across my shoulders. We agreed to try living apart for a time, although we knew this was less a trial than a prelude to our dissolution.

Ezra moved in to a small apartment up by the park and wanted to be free to see other people. He'd always been very sexual. I didn't want to know about any of it, but eventually he told me when he came round to take care of the plants, and I didn't interrupt him. The years fell away quickly, and we saw each other often; we were never out of each other's lives. In many ways we grew closer again, confiding in each other once more, or, that is to say, he told me about the women he saw, none very seriously; I tended to tell him about my clients and projects. Ezra didn't earn much as the assistant manager of the local bookstore, so I helped him out occasionally when he let me. He traveled with me to both of my parents' funerals nine months apart. We met for dinner regularly, a movie sometimes. I cooked for him, he cooked for me. But I didn't take him to dinner parties or events as my plus-one; he didn't spend time with my friends. When we met up, it was always only the two of us. I never felt as centered as I did when I was driving back to the house on the hill after being in his company.

Whenever Ezra was involved with someone, we saw each other less. During these periods, I missed him but wanted him to settle down with someone new in a meaningful way. Only then would I be able to pursue my own happiness, then it would be my time; I can see now this was my thinking. The longest I'd ever gone without hearing from him was two weeks.

Two months ago in September, I hadn't heard from Ezra for three weeks. I was busier than usual working on the conversion of a landmark insurance headquarters into a charter school. Something had happened between us—I won't go into it—and I was trying to achieve some distance. When Ezra didn't answer a series of texts, I thought, Well, I hope I like her.

Another week went by, and he still wasn't answering my texts or calls, and I became worried. I dropped by his apartment. When I was knocking on his door, the property manager stepped out and said she assumed Ezra had gone away because he had missed his rent. This was very unusual. Weirdly though his car was still in his garage— she'd checked that morning. Ezra had known some dark days, and I didn't think his depression ever became so unbearable that he'd harm himself, but I panicked. I had my key out before the property manager grabbed hers.

The wool blanket I'd given him for his last birthday was neatly folded across his made bed. Pillars of art books doubled as night tables. Ezra's clothes, shoes, and luggage were in his closet. He had always been neat. The dishes were put away, but there were some salad greens going bad in the refrigerator. There was a stack of bills and magazines on his writing desk along with a fat biography of a poet bisected by a bookmark and a mug marked by rings of evaporated coffee. And next to the mug and the book was a printout of an article: it was the essay that had launched the stranger game.

THE DAY AFTER I'D FOLLOWED THE WOMAN AND CHILD
home from the park, I went into the office early to work
on some renderings but had difficulty focusing. For a
change of scenery, I walked to the museum at noon
and slipped into an exhibition of recent acquisitions by
younger artists. The very first patrons I noticed were
two men standing in front of an expansive abstract painting of layered squares, off-whites floating over delicate
blues floating over earthy browns. The work looked
like a painting but was actually a collage of ephemera—
boarding passes, sales receipts, postcards, circulars—all of
which were sanded into one smooth plane and drenched
in resin. It was unusually beautiful. I observed the two
men. One was tall, scantily bearded, wearing steel glasses;
the other was younger, tightly packed into his sweater
and slacks. Both of them admired the work, too, as far

as I could tell. I stepped closer and stood with my back to them, facing a kanji-shaped cardboard sculpture.

The taller and older man solicited the younger man's reaction: What did he see? A landscape, the younger one said. Hills rising in the distance, like when one looked north in the city—do you see it? Hills spackled with low-lying homes. He speculated about how it was made, and the older one recalled something useful about decoupage, then chuckled. He said he didn't know what he was talking about, he was talking out of his ass, which (I noticed when I looked over my shoulder) prompted the younger one to pat the taller man's behind. They were new lovers, I decided, and it was the younger one's idea to spend a day off at the museum because the older one had written in his dating profile that he felt equally at home in museums and sports arenas, and the younger one had said, Well, let's see about that. Should we start with an exhibit or go to a basketball game?

They continued holding hands as they shifted left toward the next work. I slipped in front of the collage. The younger man had a way of tipping back his head in laughter no matter what the older man said. The older man—older by fifteen years?—gestured with his free hand, making ever-wider enthusiastic circles and then, suddenly, pointing at one corner of a photograph. The younger man was looking first at his new boyfriend, then the sleepy portrait of a teenager slouching back on a bike seat. These roles were fine for now, mentor and acolyte, but what would the younger man teach the older one to keep things even? Here, listen to this song, I love this band. Hey, let's go camping in the desert next weekend, you did say you'd go camping.

The men were quiet when it was only the three of us in the elevator, me staring the whole time at my shoes, and I wondered if with this proximity I was breaking the no-contact rule, even though I said nothing, never met their glance, and preserved a safe distance following them out of the building and into the courtyard. I waited one stoplight cycle before crossing the street after them and assumed I'd lose them, but they were easy to find checking out the food trucks, settling on the one selling healthy salads. I didn't actually want the sesame noodles I bought one truck over.

There wasn't anywhere to sit, so the two men crossed back to the museum plaza and perched at the edge of a planter. For now they were protected in new romance, but maybe the older one had been single so long, he'd become set in his ways, and he was annoyed by a flaw he'd observed lately in the younger man, that he refused to acknowledge when he didn't know enough about a topic (especially politics), because he probably thought expressing a strong opinion was better than offering no opinion. All of our lives were chaptered, which the older man knew well enough; maybe the younger man did, too. But if the older man was writing his fourth or fifth chapter, and the younger only his second, would they last together?

Memories now: Ezra and I making out in an apple orchard when we were twenty-four. Napping in the afternoon in a hotel abroad, a late plate of pasta, red wine, willfully getting lost in the canal city at night. Ezra the easily distracted sous chef unevenly dicing shallots, more interested in amusing me with an account of his day, the crazies who had come into the store, how he'd write them into the novel he'd never finish because there was always so much to add. Ezra coaxing James the Cat down from our one tall tree in front (James was first my cat, then our cat)—Ezra cradling James toward the end, knowing we'd have to put the poor guy down. Ezra the troubled sleeper, slipping back into bed after a four a.m. neighborhood walk, thinking I wouldn't notice, but how could I not notice? I'd pull his right arm over me and hold it and say, You're not going anywhere now—

My phone vibrated in my pocket, our studio assistant reminding me about the conference call with contractors that I was now late for. And then I noticed the older man staring over at me. I was playing the game all wrong. I had neglected my subjects. I hadn't observed them closely enough to forge a connection. They remained elusive, and instead of trying to achieve greater empathy, I had waded into my own reverie.

As I headed toward the street, I looked back one more time: the two men were standing now, giggling about something, the younger one tipping back his head, the older one with his right hand pressed flat against the younger man's stomach, then patting his abdomen. You, you're impossible, come on, let's get you something else to eat, and I could use a glass of chardonnay—what? It is *not* too early. Let's get you a sandwich and both of us some wine and we can sit and watch everyone go by— now, how does that sound?

THE ESSAY I FOUND ON EZRA'S DESK HAD RUN EIGH-
teen months earlier in an online journal known for its
literary travel writing, much of which was posted by
guest contributors. It immediately went viral. Usually
the articles were accounts of glacier hikes or reef dives;
there were columns about what to see when you only
had three days in a river city, that sort of thing. This
particular essay—the author's bio stated only "A. Craig
is a pseudonym"—read unlike any other filed under the
rubric *Road Trips*. It was titled "Perro Perdido."

> Late in the autumn of my life, I came to the realization that I
> did not like myself very much. I had been teaching literature
> at the same college for thirty years and not written a new
> lecture in half that time, my disengagement only surpassed
> by that of my students. For many years my research sustained
> me, but the midcentury realist authors whom I once cher-

ished and to whom I was forever linked as a scholar had become odious tenants whom I seemed unable to evict. My romantic life was likewise jejune. My very last affair ended unceremoniously while driving home from a party. I was doing what I always did, which was to run through all of the new people whom we'd met, issuing an acerbic group critique. The too-tight skirts, the pop politics, the overall idiocy and decline of serious reading. I was especially good (I thought) at mimicking voices and was mocking someone's recitation of her weekly cleansing routine when my girlfriend said, Stop it, please. Why do you always have to be so mean about everyone? But I'm only trying to amuse you, I said. Well, stop it, my girlfriend said, it's getting old. But I pushed it and said, Oh, come on, you love it when I— No, she said. I don't know why I ever encouraged you. Stop, please, she yelled again. I said stop! By which she meant stop the car. I'm suffocating, she said, I need air. She got out and walked off into the darkness. I never saw her again.

So I found no fulfillment in my work, experienced increasingly briefer runs at dating, and also diagnosed myself as the kind of snob I'd loathed as a younger man. Jogging in the park in the morning, I became inordinately irked by the women who nattered away on their cell phones while speed-walking, by the men who wore sunglasses even when it was cloudy; I found myself interrupting colleagues during meetings to correct their pronunciation of ex officio (It's Latin—with a hard C, please); I looked down on the drivers

of luxury sedans and mothers in parks with sloppy toddlers
and overweight people eating ice cream.

The truth was I was achingly lonesome. I would come home
to the house I'd once upon a time hoped to share with a life-
long lover and keep as few lights on as possible to avoid
feeling overwhelmed by the rooms that needed repainting
and the warped cabinets and the general lack of wall art.
How lonely and alone I was, drinking, masturbating, drinking more until I fell asleep in front of cooking shows. At
least in the morning I had my routine, somewhere I needed
to be, a position of some respect. Then the worst possible
thing happened: I came up for a sabbatical, and because
I was entitled to it, I took it.

I winced when I read about Craig's relationship to his
house. It was easy enough to picture him padding around
empty rooms, with too many hours he couldn't fill, with
no plan for his time away from his college. He wrote that
he slept in later and later each day. He started going to
neighborhoods in the city where he wouldn't run into
anyone he knew and where he could sit in cafés for hours
and solve crosswords. He noticed he wasn't the only one
in any given coffee shop staring at a book without turning the pages. When he stopped off at the grocery store
on the way home, he stood in silent confederacy with
the other people purchasing single portions of lasagna
from the deli. This, too, sounded familiar.

One evening, Craig continued, he realized that be-

sides ordering his coffee from a barista, his only interaction of the day was helping a woman retrieve a box of
chocolate chip cookies from a top shelf, and it occurred
to him, given how chatty she was, that quite possibly it
was also one of the few interactions she'd had, as well.

It made no sense. A city full of people: Why was there loneliness everywhere I looked?

The next day I walked down the hill from my house to a
taco stand on the boulevard. My order was ready right at
the same time as the one put in by a young woman, and I
took a step back and pretended to inspect the contents of
the bag I had been handed, although what I was doing was
staring at her, unable to avert my gaze. She was wearing
a plaid jacket, a striped skirt of an entirely different palette,
and leggings printed with an animal pattern. What a mess.
And, oh, her hair; her hair was a feathery fuchsia that reminded me of one of those trolls you hoped you didn't get
when you inserted a coin in a boardwalk vending machine—

Stop it, I told myself (hearing my ex-girlfriend in my mind).
Why did I need to be so dismissive? The woman had style,
or a style, and maybe (no, definitely) it didn't appeal to me,
yet she probably liked the way she looked or she wouldn't
be parading around in this outfit, drawing the gaze, I noticed as she walked away, of both a man walking a spaniel and the spaniel.

I followed her.

She had perfect posture, a dancer's line. Her feet were turned out while she waited for a light to change. Where did she get the self-confidence to put herself together like this?

Even though she was holding the bag with her tacos in it, the woman turned into a vintage dress store. I stood on the sidewalk but watched her inside examining a long beaded frock (quite a different look than what she had on). I pretended to be looking at my phone when she exited the store and continued down the block. I followed her past a vegan café, past another boutique. She went into a store that sold barware and pricey liquor. This time I went in, too, and pretended to sort through an ice bucket full of novelty stirrers. The woman headed straight for the bourbon in the back. She asked a clerk for help—her voice was a round alto, and she had an accent: Could you by chance recommend a good earthy bourbon?

Then she finally glanced over at me ever so briefly, long enough for me to notice her eyes, pure sapphire, and I thought if you're born with eyes that vivid, you will probably be attracted to bold color your whole life. I wanted to keep following her, but what if she saw that I was also carrying a bag from the taco stand? I did not want her to feel like I was stalking her even if that was exactly what I was doing.

I thought about her all afternoon. Had she come to this country alone? Did she have someone in her life with whom she could share tacos? Carnitas for you, pollo for me. What color was *his* hair? How did *he* dress? I decided she had done some modeling because she was tall and her look probably held marketable appeal. But the modeling career, it was a sideline, a way to earn money while she pursued her greater ambition—which was what? I could make up something: she wanted to front an all-girl band, she wanted to get a psychology degree and work with at-risk teens—but the truth was I didn't have enough information to get a sense of who she was in the world. At first I'd wanted to write her off because she looked clownish, but now I yearned to connect to her, however tentatively, even at a distance.

Let's mark this as the moment when I recognized that a transformation in my life was not only possible, but also, remarkably, within my reach.

The day after following the fuchsia-haired woman, Craig walked down the hill to the taco stand at approximately the same time, although he knew the chances were slim that he'd find her again. Instead someone else caught his attention, two people, an elderly couple across the street. The man was quite bundled up given the warm weather, a sweater pulled high around his neck, and he moved stiffly around a small cherry of a car to where the woman was standing. It seemed reasonable to assume they were married. The woman appeared both serene and distant. She was wearing a knit cap. She didn't look the man in the eye when he opened the passenger-

side door for her and eased her into the seat. Craig noted
the tenderness with which the man, still moving very
slowly, reached across the woman to buckle her safety
belt. Then the man took half an eternity to walk around
the car and slip in behind the wheel. Eventually he sped
off, and not at a pace commensurate with his mobility;
he drove fast, dangerously fast, as if with the potential
speed of the car, the man were compensating for his di-
minished agility. This sporty coupe, impractically low
to the ground, devilishly bright, was affirmatively alive
with horsepower.

> At home that night, I found myself thinking only about the
> fuchsia-haired woman and the sports car couple, and I ex-
> perienced the pleasant erasure of time that I always imag-
> ined writers must enjoy when they submerged themselves
> in their characters. But eventually my own solitude returned.
> How faint and spectral I looked to myself reflected in the
> window. I didn't want to become a ghost. I knew I needed
> to get out and wander. This was how I came up with my
> scheme, rules and all.

I imagine that given what A. Craig subsequently
started doing, no matter the boundaries he set and no
matter his intent in posting this so-called travelogue, he
knew most readers would consider him little more than
a sketchy voyeur; thus the pseudonym. His first real follow (his term) involved driving across the city and slip-

ping into a table at a boardwalk café, the ocean loud on the other side of the wide white beach.

It was sunny out, and there were volleyball games in progress, skaters in slalom around tourists, sunbathers, and most important a crowd ample enough for me to become one more nobody. I ordered a sandwich and coffee and watched a group form around a gray-haired older woman wearing a red bikini and performing what might be described as an exotic dance; a muscular, significantly younger man with a boom box hoisted up on his shoulder moved in a circle around her. I focused on one woman in a purple dress standing at the edge of the group and taking in the spectacle. That I picked out this person at random and stuck with her was part of my plan.

When she began continuing her walk south down the boardwalk, I left cash on the table and followed her, moving quickly out of the touristy commercial stretch into a neighborhood of beach houses and walk streets. The crowd had thinned, and so I had a better view of her, but I also became more conspicuous, especially when she abruptly came to a halt and I had to stop, too, with nothing to duck behind.

The woman had spotted a cat basking in the sun. The cat was round, cared for, orange, on its back. And docile: it neither righted itself nor skittered off when the woman bent down to pet it. After a few good strokes, the woman pulled something from a tote bag, which caused the cat to flip around onto all fours and sit back on its haunches. The cat dug his snout into the woman's open palm and devoured what must have been a treat. When the woman stood, she waited while the cat rubbed up against her legs.

I maintained an even distance as the woman turned into a block of bungalows. A few houses in, she saw a gray cat lying out on a broad porch, and she walked right up the front path to pet this one, too, a cat who also did not run away, who also eagerly accepted the woman's caresses and eventual treat. Among these cats, she apparently enjoyed renown. Around the corner, yet another one appeared to be guarding a local election sign planted in the lawn; he received the same treatment. Two blocks east, the woman ministered her affections to a fat black Persian. Having slipped behind an easement eucalyptus, I was close enough to hear her friendly lilt, but not close enough to hear what exactly she said.

I hadn't been in this part of town in a while and didn't know it well, and the farther from the beach the woman strolled, the tighter the plot of streets became. When she turned a corner, I lost her. Maybe she went inside. I'd decided that my random follow needed to be conducted without the benefit of technology, but ultimately I did take out my phone to pull up a map. I'd had no contact with the woman, and I was pretty sure I had eluded detection (and therefore not caused alarm), so for the greater part I'd obeyed my own rules.

This had been interesting. Here was a cat lady who had a routine, a neighborhood; she belonged somewhere, but I didn't know anything else about her, like if she herself had cats. Maybe she couldn't because she lived her life with someone allergic to them, so she distributed her affections elsewhere. Or maybe she did live with cats and had extra love and treats to spare. I had no sense of how she'd spend her afternoon. Would her evening be as solitary as mine? Like me, did she have too much time to think? I accepted I'd never know. The final rule I'd made for myself was in many ways the most important; which was that if I tried to follow the same person twice, I might be perceived of as a threat.

I wanted to be extra sure I went unseen, so the next day I started following strangers by car. Maybe it wasn't true, but I thought I'd be less noticeable driving and able to get away faster if I was discovered. I drove over the hill into the valley, to a development of white stucco houses with red tile roofs. I coasted around awhile, not spotting anyone, and then I saw a woman loading three children into a minivan. Where were they going at eleven in the morning on a school day?

I stayed with the minivan on a six-lane boulevard, even though the driver didn't believe in using her turn signal. I worked out a scenario: the kids attended a parochial school, and today was a religious holiday, but the woman wasn't pious and she'd promised to take them out for lunch some-where fun, a diner where the waiters all sang if it was your birthday, a bowling alley, something like that. I could see the kids in the back of the minivan were a wild bunch, bouncing up and down, jabbing each other. Or maybe what was actually going on was dark: she was one of those evil mothers whose tale was told too late; she'd snapped and was going to drive the minivan off a bridge and kill them all in one sudden swerve—weren't they now headed toward a bridge that spanned the freeway? Should I call 911?

No need. Where they ended up about ten miles later was on another sun-flattened street not unlike the one they'd started out on. A man roughly the same age as the woman stepped out onto his stoop. I parked across the street and unrolled my window. I could hear lively pop music emanating from the man's house. The man stayed put while the woman slid open the door to the minivan. The children poured out and shuffled toward the house. The man went inside with the kids, and then the woman was back in the minivan, pulling away.

No wonder the kids were anxious: they should have been in school but were forced instead to perform this custodial dance. Would the father get them to their soccer practices and guitar lessons? The woman, meanwhile, doubled back the way we'd come. She pulled into a strip mall. I waited a moment, then followed her into a crafts store. One wall was devoted to yarn, which was where the woman stood and ran her fingertips across soft skeins. She was getting ideas, she told the salesperson. Was she knitting a gift for someone? Probably, the woman said, she usually gave away what she made. She had family somewhere cold. At night, especially when her ex-husband had the kids, it helped to keep her hands busy.

The woman actually didn't speak any of this—these were my thoughts—but I wanted to imagine her life. I wanted to lose myself in it. And was I correct about her? Did it matter? Something was breaking in me, and after I left the store and went a short ways, I had to pull over because I became too teary to drive. Did I feel sorry for the woman? Not exactly, but I recognized a pattern: I projected loneliness onto everyone whom I encountered. The stories I was concocting, they were in the end all about me, weren't they? And I desperately needed to move beyond the perimeter of my own being.

I drove around some more with no clue where I was, and I followed other people: gardeners trimming coral trees, an old woman walking an old dachshund, three young guys tossing a basketball back and forth. I would follow one person or group for a while, then veer off and follow another: a carom follow.

Back home I took a warm shower. It must have been nine or ten at night, and I'd not eaten. I was so exhausted that I sat down in the stall with the water beating down on my shoulders. How was it possible I'd lost sight of what bound humans to one another? The same epic sorrows, the same epic joys. I had to wonder how alone I was in drifting so easily from such basic commune, and maybe this was more common than I realized. If nothing else at this point, I understood how terribly un-unique I was.

I couldn't figure out where Craig was headed. He seemed at once to be making discoveries and to be riding a downward slope into deeper despondency. When he left his house in the mornings, he brought snack bars and sandwiches, a change of shirt, a sweater. He followed one person or group of people and then the next, and when he lost the light and wanted to head home, sometimes he had to drive an hour, an hour and a half through traffic from a neighboring county. He wanted to see how far he could push this, how far from home he was willing to go, how lost he was willing to get. This went on for a month, and then one morning he prepared for a longer road trip.

Since I wasn't sure where I was heading, into what climate, I packed a bag with both cargo shorts and a cardigan. I drove across the river into the eastern part of the city and tracked a food truck. I caromed off into a park in pursuit of some of the food truck customers and watched them picnic. From the park, I picked up a pack of motorcyclists heading east, and this took me some distance into drier terrain.

The road threaded through mustard-colored towns, past silos, past windmills. I stopped at a diner somewhere and watched four women chat over lunch. I followed one of them to a storefront dance studio. There was a locksmith finishing up a task there—I followed him out on another a call. And so on. Trees disappeared, there was only rough scrub, then little of that.

In the desert, one hundred and fifty miles from home, I ran out of daylight and stopped at a motel. I fell asleep in my clothes. The next morning, I followed motel guests after they checked out, a man and a woman about my age. They were portly in the same way, both wearing jeans, cowboy shirts, boots, and I decided they were a couple who over time had grown to look alike the way couples do; it was also possible they were siblings.

I stayed with them on the highway and exited when they did an hour later, each new desert town more baked than the last. I worried they had noticed me, and I dropped back, letting their car push forward until it was no bigger than a hawk hugging the horizon.

Without warning the car pulled off the road, sending up a cloud of dust, and wound down a dirt drive toward a ranch house. They parked next to two pickups, one of them up on blocks. Tempted though I was, I couldn't very well drive down the dirt road, too, and I couldn't stay parked up on the street. I wanted to know what the couple/siblings were up to—there had been something notably joyless about them when they'd left the motel without banter, grim-faced, probably not on holiday—and to figure them out, I'd have to take my chances and come back later under the cover of night to see if they were still here.

I drove around. I noticed a sign for an inn a few miles east but napped instead in my car. It started to get dark. I went back to the ranch house. The couple's car was where they'd left it. I continued a quarter mile on, parked on the shoulder, and walked back. There were lights on in the house. The property wasn't fenced, but I made sure not to get too close. I wasn't at all prepared for the desert wind, which numbed my ears. When it was truly night, I could see better into the house, and I crouched down there a long, long while, and this was what I observed:

Three people, the man and woman I'd followed (siblings after all, I decided), both moving about a kitchen, plus a white-haired man seated at the table, the man small in his chair. Their father, from the look of it. The woman was setting the table, and she tied a bib around her father's neck. The son was at the stove, spooning the contents of various pots into serving bowls. Steam rose from a bowl of spaghetti. Then the siblings sat on either side of the older man, and they held hands in grace. I heard a crescendo of laughter, and the son served food to the father, the daughter promptly cutting it up. The father couldn't feed himself; his children took turns spooning him dinner. He slumped a bit in his chair, but the siblings were merry anyway, putting on a show, telling stories.

That was it, that was all I saw, adult siblings being tender with their frail father. Where was their mother? Had she died some time ago or did she live (had she lived) another life elsewhere? The father stayed out here far from town, from other houses, so who tended to him when his adult children were not around? Was this visit routine or was it a special occasion? I waited for a birthday cake, but there was no cake, only alps of ice cream. What was the history of this family? Had there been a period of estrangement? Had a mother's final illness yielded a rapprochement? Had the siblings moved out of the desert the moment they could, or was it the father who'd fled the city? Maybe it was the siblings themselves who had been at odds, but their father's failing health had necessitated them setting aside their differences...

My lower back ached from hovering in one place for too long; the wind left me with a ringing in my ears; my hands were shaking. I drove slowly, following the signs to the nearby inn, and before I stepped inside I noticed a flyer taped up to a utility pole, and on the flyer an image of a small dog with pointy tufted ears. Across the top of the page, someone had written *Perro perdido*.

When I stepped inside the inn, I was delirious with hunger and melancholy, and to the woman who set down her book to greet me, I asked, Are there generally a lot of lost dogs in this town?

The woman thought about it. Not particularly, she said. Now and then, I suppose.

Are they ever found, the dogs that do go missing?

The woman shrugged. Some, she said. That's the hope.

That is the hope, I said.

When I asked if there was a room available, the woman of course wanted to know for how long, but I didn't have an answer. Then for some reason she asked if I was looking for work, because she was only filling in and they needed a new night manager. Was I qualified?

I wrote this essay over a series of slow nights at the front desk. I have turned my sabbatical into an extended leave, and although I suspect one day I might return to my city life, I am in no hurry. I no longer follow strangers, but I do interact with new guests at the inn every day, and when someone wants to find the old turquoise mine or a desert trail head, even if it's the morning and the end of my shift, I usher the guests where they want to go. Along the way, I try to find out as much about them as I can, what brought them here, what they are escaping and/or to what they eventually will return. Where they are headed next.

Once upon a time I was an avid traveler and left the country twice a year. I used to keep a checklist of places I needed to see, the monuments, the landscapes. Now I am less interested in places than people. I can't get enough of people.

I very much doubt that most of you reading my account have or will become as closed off as I did, as cold at night, as folded inward, but for those of you who do worry that you, too, might slide into similar despair, I suggest you study the nearest stranger from a safe distance and watch him or her a long while.

Forget about yourself. Don't make an approach. This is your only chance. Look. Keep looking.

How can you draw a line connecting you and this stranger? How can you make that line indelible?

THE FIRST QUESTIONS THE INVESTIGATING DETECTIVE asked me about the last time I'd seen Ezra were the obvious ones: Had he appeared restless or preoccupied? Was he evasive about anything? Did he seem manic? Or hopeless?

"Did Mr. Voight say anything cryptic?" Detective Martinez asked.

Not that I could recall. The last time I'd been with him was on a Sunday. I was dropping off a cast-iron skillet—

"A skillet?" the detective asked. "Why a skillet?"

There was one in my kitchen that was especially good for searing. I was eating out or ordering in all the time, whereas Ezra had been on a cooking jag. When I showed up he was already making mushroom risotto. I was instructed to pour myself a glass of wine, have a seat, and keep him company while he stirred in wine and broth.

"He seemed settled," the detective said. "In a good place."

"I don't know. Maybe that's what I wanted to see," I said.

The risotto was loamy and rich, and we shared a bottle of the same wine he'd cooked with. Ezra was excited about an art book he'd purchased. Even with his employee discount, he spent too much on books, but I didn't say anything. It was a monograph of an artist we'd both long admired, plates of prints made over the years when this artist wasn't producing the monumental sculpture she was better known for. In pencil, she would cover a page with notations, numbers, a schematic drawing that looked like a blueprint or a plan for an imaginary city, and then within the grids and boxes, across her notations, she would lay in geometric blocks in powdery pigment, one bold color per print, usually cadmium orange. She made the same kind of work again and again for years, and as we were sitting next to each other on Ezra's couch, the book open on his lap, what he remarked on, what he found extraordinary, was the way an artist might latch on to an idiom early in a career, and his or her whole output for decades would become variations on an initial theme. But the work never got dull—the opposite. It only grew subtler, more sublime. There was the sculptor with his steel plates, the composer with his arpeggios, the author with her driving declarative refrains. How did they know at such an early age that they were on to something? Where did that self-confidence come from? It's so alien to me and you, Ezra said.

"To me and *you*?" the detective asked. "I can understand him speaking for himself, but why did he include you?"

Detective Martinez had an uncanny way of not blinking until her question was answered. She had zeroed in on my discomfort right away.

"When Ezra and I were younger," I told her, "he wanted to be a novelist, and I was going to be an artist. Off and on, he was still working on something, but I stopped painting after college—"

"You gave up on it."

"I was never very good at it. I'd have a picture of something in my mind, but then anything I made fell far short of that image. But painting led me to art history, which led to architectural history, and when I imagined becoming an architect, I became so much happier."

"But Ezra thought you'd left something behind," Detective Martinez said. "Maybe he thought that *you* thought he should likewise give up his writing, too—"

"No. I always encouraged him."

"Earn a real living—"

"You're putting words in my mouth," I said.

Ezra used to say that there were two kinds of people: those who looked completely different when they had wet hair, and those who looked exactly the same when their hair was wet or dry. For some reason he never explained, he didn't trust the people whose hair looked the same wet or dry. The detective likely fell in that category.

"It's my job to come up with a line and follow that line," she said. "I don't always get it right. Then I try to find a better line. It's an imperfect method, I admit."

I accepted her apology, if that was what it was, with a nod.

"So you stayed for dinner and were looking at this art book, and he suggested that you and he were alike in your inability to realize your dreams, even if that wasn't an accurate representation of the situation for you."

I could have pointed out that for every artist who found his voice early on, there was the genius who created great work later in life. Plus Ezra and I were not that old—maybe no longer young, but only forty. He had time. But I didn't say these things that night.

"And that was that," Detective Martinez said. "Nothing else happened?"

I didn't answer.

"Ms. Crane?"

"We talked some more, but yes, that was that," I said.

Detective Martinez was staring at me again without blinking. She knew I was lying. I glanced around her office, void of personal effects. No photos, no mementos.

"I keep thinking about a documentary we saw," I said. "It was about a man who disappeared and was found a month later at a hospital not too far from home, but without any ID. He had amnesia. No one would ever figure out what triggered it. The only thing he had with him was a book with a phone number scribbled on the inside cover, which belonged to an ex-girlfriend. She was traveling and unreachable. When she finally came home, she was able to identify the man. The man had retained the ability to do physical things, like ride a bike or surf or make love—even speak French. But he remembered no people or places or experiences. The first time he saw snow after his amnesia, he was both awestruck like a child might be, and analytic like an adult, trying to figure out what it consisted of."

"Amnesia is pretty rare."

"Oh, I wasn't suggesting—"

"Mr. Voight liked this film?"

"He saw it several times when it came out."

The detective wrote this down, although I didn't know how it would be useful. Then she set down her pen and laced her fingers.

She said, "Mr. Voight has been gone only one month, but—"

"*Only* one month?"

"But you need to consider the possibility that he doesn't want to be found."

"You're saying you don't think we'll find him?" I asked.

"No," she said. "I'm saying it's possible he doesn't want you to find him."

This was a sharp arrow; it went in deep. I already knew

that, yes. How could I not have thought about that? She didn't need to say it aloud, not yet anyway.

"I'll start in on the databases right away," Detective Martinez said, softer. "Let's see if we can learn anything."

Protocols were followed: I provided photos, descriptions of physical attributes (including the location of the moles along Ezra's chin that his scruff usually masked), and lists of friends and relatives (although like me, he wasn't close to his family). I filled out an exhaustive questionnaire about what he might be wearing and carrying in the leather shoulder bag that we could say was missing, and per Detective Martinez's request, I arranged to have his dental records sent over. I dropped off a pair of shoes, too. That part was disconcerting, walking into the precinct with my right index and middle fingers hooked into the heels of Ezra's worn chukkas, like I was cleaning up after him and returning his things to our closet.

Meanwhile the detective was funneling information into the web of databases operated by various agencies and hospital systems—and morgues. I tried not to think about the morgues. I could access his bank account because he hadn't changed his password since college, but I could see he wasn't withdrawing cash. (I'd started paying his rent because I didn't want to move his belongings to my house; that seemed to suggest he'd never be found or never come back.) According to the bookstore, he had cashed his last paycheck, so he had some money. (At the bookstore, they thought he'd quit without giving notice, which was out of character, but plausible.) We tracked his credit cards, but he wasn't using them. He wasn't using his cell phone either. He didn't appear on any closed-circuit cameras in local shopping malls or major intersections. He'd never much tapped into social media. I was supposed to tell my friends and colleagues about what was going on to cast a wider net, and I did; they weren't surprised Ezra would pull a stunt like this— a stunt, as if his disappearance were a performance. The detective wanted me to post flyers. Perro perdido, please wander home. I didn't end up posting anything, and besides, the police had already canvassed nearby shop owners and neighbors about whether they'd seen him.

After a month (which meant Ezra had been missing for two), I showed up at the police station unannounced and demanded to see Detective Martinez. She met me at the front desk because she had someone in her office and guided me to a free bench.

"I haven't heard anything from you in weeks," I said.

"Rebecca—"

"You haven't taken me seriously this whole time. You've implied more than once that there's something peculiar about my history with Ezra."

"I don't think I ever said anything like that."

"I don't think you've been harnessing the full force of the department to find him."

People waiting to be called to pay citations and report petty thefts all stared at me. For some reason, this was the moment I noticed that Detective Martinez's earlobes were both multiply pierced, although she wore no jewelry.

She leaned toward me and whispered, "I think we both know you haven't been completely straight with me."

Now I was the one who didn't blink.

"For whatever reason, you decided not to tell me what you found when you first went into Ezra's apartment with the property manager," she said.

I blinked.

"I'm guessing the property manager noticed me taking the printout," I said.

"Look," Detective Martinez said, "this stranger game is the bane of my existence. Do you know how many missing persons reports have been filed in the last year alone?"

"Stranger game?" I asked.

"The article. You read it?"

"Yes, but what about it?"

"The fad that came out of it," Detective Martinez said. "You mean to say you don't know about that?"

I shook my head no.

"That's refreshing," the detective said. "I wish more people didn't know about it. But then why did you take the article with you?"

I'd sensed it was important. I wanted to know what Ezra was reading when he vanished. He'd always had a way of being deeply affected by whatever he encountered, be it a book, a song, a dog, a tree—he was both more available than I was to be influenced and more readily buffeted.

"It's been passed around five million times, ten million times," the detective said. "I don't think we really know how many times."

She described the craze the essay had launched, and I was confused.

"But the article is about overcoming your alienation," I said.

"I think most people only read about the other people playing the game, not the original article itself."

"It's a terrible misinterpretation then. There is no mention of any kind of *game*."

"The writer talks about empathy, but the game isn't about that at all. It's about seeing how long you can follow a stranger without getting caught. There are the three rules because it wouldn't be a game without rules. But it's not a game at all. From where I sit, it's called stalking."

Some gossip I'd heard about a friend of a friend now made sense. This person was an ambitious associate at a big law firm, the consummate networker, and meanwhile always planning weekend getaways with her fiancé. But some months ago, she had become deeply engaged in an activity that my friend labeled addictive. I assumed it was drugs. Then my friend's friend started showing up late to meetings and went missing for hours, and apparently she lied to her fiancé about her whereabouts—the fiancé assumed she was hiding an affair. It didn't let up. Eventually the fiancé left her and the woman was asked to take a leave from her law firm to sort things out; she'd moved in with her mother, but by all accounts, she still went missing for days at a time. When I asked my friend what kind of drugs her friend had gotten into, or if it was alcohol, my friend made it clear there weren't substances involved; her friend had been *playing the game*, and I assumed *game* was code for gambling or sex.

"So people lose themselves in this," I said. "But do they usually disappear?"

"Eventually they come home, they turn up," Detective Martinez said. "It's a waste of our resources chasing grown adults who run off one day because they feel like it, but we don't choose who we look for and who we don't. We look for everybody."

I very much could see the appeal to Ezra. He craved the open road, and he took so much pleasure in meeting strangers. He quizzed taxi drivers and airplane row mates and buskers in the park for their life stories.

"I separated from my husband last year after twenty years," Detective Martinez said. "We met on the force. I still work with him. We get along fine, all things considered. We have joint custody of the dogs. So I understand how things might be between you and Ezra. The concern, the care—it doesn't simply stop. You could've told me about finding the article."

I was still very much in love with Ezra, and the detective was probably still very much in love with her soon-to-be ex-husband, and the whole world was full of people very much in love with lost lovers. We sat there a moment longer before the detective stood up to return to whomever was in her office, and I pulled her arm so she sat back down.

I wanted to ask: Have you ever watched someone close to you slip away? You see it happening, but there's nothing you can do about it—has that happened to you?

Instead I said, "He was always a little adrift. It was charming for a while, and then it was exhausting." I said, "I didn't take care of him."

I started sobbing in my hands, and the detective's whole posture changed. She slumped back in the bench a bit. When I looked up, I noticed everyone in the room doing his or her best to look away.

"I live around the corner from here. I made chicken soup last night. Come home with me now, I'll give you some homemade soup, you'll feel better. Let me get rid of the people in my office, then we'll get you some soup."

"This sounds unorthodox," I said.

"Nobody follows the rules all the time," the detective said.

Her house was a clapboard cottage painted mint green, the trim also green but darker. Green was clearly Detective Martinez's favorite color because her sunlit cozy kitchen with its shelves of cookbooks and pots hanging over the range was yet another soft green. I did feel calmer sipping warm soup on a warm day. There was a collection of frogs on a windowsill, some crystal, some plastic. Two large dogs were lolling in the sun in the backyard. I knew that Detective Martinez didn't want to tell me that after two months she was pretty sure Ezra wouldn't turn up. She wasn't exactly my new friend, but she knew I needed a new friend.

"Can I ask you something?" Detective Martinez said. "And I ask this because I'm trying to help. You admitted to finding the article, great. Is there anything else maybe that you haven't told me?"

"Nothing," I said a little too quickly.

The detective didn't blink.

"Now you know everything," I said.

"Okay. Right."

"No, honestly, you do."

"All right then, I'll believe you. Let me put it this way. Rebecca, let's say hypothetically that Ezra *has* moved on—"

"I haven't been to the studio today," I said. "I really should go."

"Let's just say he's moved on. You two haven't been together awhile now. Let's just say he disappeared because he wanted a new life, and this was the only way he knew how to find it. So. What about you? What are you going to do now for *yourself*?"

I wasn't going to give the detective what she wanted. I thanked her for her soup and sympathy, told her to let me know if she learned anything new, and I left.

A MEMORY NOW, A WINTER NIGHT—EZRA AND I
tucked into opposite corners of the couch. I might have
been half reading a novel, half staring out at the city,
considering getting into bed, but Ezra would be up another hour or longer; he was wide-awake, elsewhere,
studying the maps of a country thousands of miles away.
He'd brought home a travel guide from the bookstore,
one from the series he liked that came packed with extra
history and excerpts by literary heroes juxtaposed with
the usual photos of spires and spice markets. We hadn't
necessarily agreed this was where we'd go the following summer, but in his mind we were on our way, and
the planning fell to him. Ezra took such pleasure in con-
structing the perfect day. We'd follow the path he'd mark
out for us, from the chapel with restored frescoes to the
house where a poet wrote his odes and died young, across
stone bridges, through a cluttered cemetery, coiling up

narrow streets until we reached the ledge of a park over-looking the jeweled city, the city a puzzle we'd solved to-gether. Then Ezra would withdraw a bottle of wine from his backpack, a wedge of cheese, bread, fruit—a sleight of hand because I never noticed him packing a picnic (or I chose not to keep track of what he was doing be-cause I wanted to be surprised). These were days of lidless pleasure. My only dread would be the return flight, the arrival home, Ezra's lassitude when we had to fall back into our regular routines. In later years when he seemed down to me, I'd ask him where we were going next to cheer him up, and this worked for a time—he'd come home with a new travel guide, he'd unfold new maps. It worked, and then it didn't work so much; nothing did.

Another memory, even earlier, from around the time Ezra moved out west to be with me. On Sunday after-noons, postnap, predinner, he would announce we were going on a drive. A drive where? I'd ask. Oh, nowhere in particular, he'd say. The idea was we'd venture out, allow ourselves to get lost, then figure out how to get back without consulting a map. I myself didn't know the neighborhoods well because I'd been working long hours and hadn't had time to explore. Let's see what we can discover, Ezra said, and usually he would steer us up into the foothills, and we'd follow the haunches and hol-lows of that terrain until we wound down to the beach. Sometimes we got out and walked on the windy bluff at dusk. Sometimes we sat in the car parked on the side of the coast road and made out like teenagers. Dusk was Ezra's favorite time of day, and mine, too; it was impossible not to believe in your eventual prosperity when the sun melted into the pacific distance and the night was still unwritten.

Eventually there were more and more Sundays when I needed to catch up on work and begged out of the drive, and Ezra didn't pout about it; he went alone. When he came home, however, he would pull me from my desk to the couch to cuddle with him. Be with me now, he'd say, and he was cute about it, and of course I gave in. I should have gone on the drives though. Even then I could see this, and I don't know why I didn't.

I thought the stranger game might be akin to getting lost in a landscape you didn't know and then finding your way back from its littoral edge, that this was the appeal to Ezra, except he hadn't come back from this drive, had he? Be with me now. I wanted to understand what he was experiencing. I was convinced he'd become a player, and I admit it made no sense, but I thought the only way to find him was to figure out where the game might lead.

Days after following the two men at the museum, I was looking for new clothes to wear for client presentations, and I ended up randomly tracking a woman my age into the men's section of a department store. She was checking out sweaters—for whom? A friend, a boyfriend, her husband? Her ex-husband? I watched her set aside several sweaters, all of them gray. Then she stood in front of a full-length mirror and tried on each one. Were they for her? Or was it indeed a holiday gift, but a major consideration was how it would fit her when she borrowed it on cool mornings after she'd spent the night? She'd look ridiculous apparently: she put on a cardigan that looked more like a robe on her. The charcoal turtle-neck she ended up purchasing became a minidress, but she didn't care. She'd be closer to him when she wore it.

Early the following morning instead of driving to the gym, I followed a guy delivering newspapers. He had terrible aim. He slung half the papers at garage doors and light posts and had to hop out of his car to redirect the papers to stoops and gates. This was his third job, he was trying to pick up extra cash to support the little girl in the back seat, belted in next to the steep pile of news-print. He wanted her to be able to take piano lessons. The more papers he delivered, the lower the pile next to his daughter, and the better her view of a neighborhood miles away from the one where they lived.

Later that afternoon, I followed another father into a diner, a father and his son; the kid wore glasses too big for his face and read a paperback while walking. He at-tacked a shared sundae with less zeal than his father; he wanted to be reading, he wanted to be in his bedroom with the door shut. The longer I watched them from across the diner, the more vivid everything became: the red of the booth glowed in a ruby wash; the boy's lenses were as clear as new window glass; in the man's face, the first striations of age appeared right as I stared at him, like cracks emerging in burning firewood. Every edge became sharper, and maybe it was the time of year, the earlier sunsets, the angled light. Or I was in the habit of observing others with greater care. I'm trying to define a state of hyperalertness. It was a tonic. I wanted to prolong it.

I ended up out at the beach. From the bluff, I watched a photographer shoot a woman in a white dress, her dress and the filter an assistant held like the twin sails of a masted boat, full and bright. I could see the many silver rings on the photographer's fingers as he twisted the lens back and forth. I could see the model's eyes (or at least I convinced myself I could), bluer than the darkening ocean. I knew what the photographer was thinking: Almost, almost—this way, keep going, almost. I knew what the model was thinking: I can give him a little more, I can seduce him, I can see through him, I have him now.

One day I broke the second rule. I was on my way to work. A tall kid, college aged, was walking along a busy road. He was wearing a full backpack, and he had a milky cat (on a leash) perched atop his shoulders and the pack. The kid hopped across one side of the road to the center island where people often asked for money, which was what he began doing. He looked so tired to me when I drove past without stopping (I had cars behind me and the light had changed), but not without hope. With my rearview mirror, I watched him reach over his shoulder to pet the cat. I wanted to know how he'd ended up here. He was estranged from his family. He'd lost his job. He'd been kicked out of a shelter because they wouldn't let him keep the cat. He was mentally unstable. He'd simply had some bad luck. But I didn't want to fall back on the same old, same old speculation to make up my own story about him, not this kid. I wanted to know who he really was.

I circled back around to make another pass, except this time I pulled to the side of the road, waited out the traffic, and jogged across to the island.

"Hi," I said.

He seemed surprised someone would join him. Was I going to encroach his turf? Would I ask for money, too?

I held out a twenty-dollar bill and said, "For you."

He took the money with little eye contact and said, "Thank you so much. Thank you, god bless."

I stood there, stupid with too many thoughts. Do you have a place to go tonight? It will be cold. Can you use that money to get something to eat? Do you need me to care for your cat for you while you find work? Useless sentiments probably.

"Would you like to pet her?" the kid asked.

He stooped a bit so I could reach the perfectly balanced cat.

"Her name is Beautiful," he said.

"She is," I said and stroked her head and back. So soft.

"Don't cry," he said.

Was I crying?

"Watch yourself crossing that traffic," he said when I turned away.

"I will," I said. "You watch yourself, too."

"Beautiful will take care of me," he said.

I broke the third rule and drove back to the same spot the next day but didn't see the tall kid and his cat. No luck the day after that. I never saw him again—I suppose he was following the rules on my behalf. Maybe this wasn't a game I should play at all; I didn't have the temperament. One was supposed to connect but not get involved. But why *not* get involved? If the link to a stranger was entirely internal, only one-way, how could it be meaningful? Was it really any connection at all?

THE NEXT DAY WHEN I WENT TO THE MUSEUM AGAIN on my lunch break, I resisted tailing two patrons wearing identical sweaters into the sculpture garden. In the grocery store later, I thought about following a teenager who appeared to be filling her cart with an inordinate quantity of ramen and rice cakes, but I didn't. I didn't want to play this game anymore. No good would come of it.

One cloudy Thursday afternoon I drove up the coast for a meeting I wasn't at all enthusiastic about: a potential client wanted to renovate the back of a beach house to expand the kitchen, family room, and deck. An unsteady economy had forced our firm to take on domestic projects and rely less on municipal competitions, and on top of this, I hadn't been productive at all since Ezra left. My partners knew what was going on, they were kind (and even suggested I take a leave), but I didn't want to disappoint them. So I followed up on a referral and did

my best to secure the job. When I left the meeting and
drove back out onto the coast road, I should have headed
left toward the city proper and my studio, but a quartet
of motorcycles tore past, and I turned right, northward
after them.

There was something mesmerizing about the way the
bikers answered the arc of the shoreline, dipping in sync
when the road banked right or left. I could see one beard
tucked into a helmet chin strap, and some long tresses
emerging like streamers from the back of another helmet, but I couldn't really get out in front of them to
guess anything about them. That was fine. I was happy
enough to find out where they were going, which five
miles later turned out to be a fish-and-chips stand surrounded by a parking lot full of other motorcycles and
vans and recreational vehicles.

I had done a good job of following the bikers this
far but lost them when I tried to find parking. Instead
I watched two men get into a black sports car, and for
a moment I thought it might be the same couple I'd
watched at the museum. There was a glint of sunlight
off the older man's steel glasses, a rip of laughter from
the younger man—was it them? If so, why were they at
this greasy fish-and-chips joint, and why when they exited the parking lot did they head north?

The road took a sharp turn around some rocks, and I
lost them briefly. Then we were on a straightaway, and
I let another car slip between us to give me a screen. It

occurred to me that finally I was more or less following strangers the way Craig ultimately had, which was to say I'd originally been after the four bikers but switched subjects—a carom follow. We drove ten miles before hitting a stretch of car dealerships and outlet stores. Maybe another five miles after that through the flat back streets of a port city. I lost the sports car, but then I caught it again where the port city ended and the highway opened up once more. The car was a polished scarab scurrying away from me, but I wasn't going to let it get away.

It began misting. I knew that pretty soon we'd reach another coastal city, a college town, but first there was a series of roads that spun off into inland valleys, and the sports car tore down one of them. The rain dissipated, but this road descended into a bowl of fog. I caught the car swinging off onto another road—by now they surely must have noticed me following them. I stayed with them.

Was Ezra even playing the stranger game? I'd made a leap. It seemed like something that would capture his imagination, and he'd have heard about the fad at the bookstore; he'd have needed to go back to the original article, but it was possible also something terrible had happened. Detective Martinez had checked the morgues and found nothing. She'd scoured the databases, nothing, no unidentified white males matching his description. I was too much the optimist to believe he was injured or worse. If I couldn't picture him harmed, then he couldn't be harmed.

Night had fallen, and we'd driven far from the coastal highway, with no houses around. It was raining now— and I lost the sports car, although it had to be out there. I reached a turnoff, a narrower gravel road. They must have taken it. The road tapered even more and curved around. I came to an abrupt stop. I was all alone out here.

With some difficulty, I managed to turn around, but when I made it back to the valley road, I wasn't clear which way to go because all of the switchbacks had left me disoriented. I didn't want to guess, I only wanted to go home, and I pulled over to find my phone, technology my only guide now (sorry, A. Craig). The rain drummed against my windshield. My phone wasn't in my bag, nor was it in a cup holder or in the glove compartment. I groped around under the seat. It wasn't anywhere to be found—oh, no. I remembered taking it out during my meeting to retrieve some contact information, and I'd left it on the table. I could picture it sitting next to the drawings I'd unfurled during my presentation.

I was furious at myself. I leaned on the horn. I needed to find the coast road. The downpour made the road slick. Oh, Ezra. I pounded the steering wheel twice with both fists, two syllables, Ezra. The last time I'd seen him, he'd made me his mushroom risotto, we drank a bottle of wine, we looked at his new monograph, the pencil and pigment prints. And that was that, Detective Martinez said. Nothing else happened? She knew I wasn't giving her the complete story.

Ezra closed the art book and set it on the end table next to the couch, and when he turned back toward me, I kissed him. He squinted at me, not so much confused, but trying to read me. I shook my head and laughed. He laughed, too. What were we doing? He parted my hair with his fingers. He leaned in, hesitated. His breath against my neck. He pulled me around, up, over him so I was straddling him. His hands slid up my sweater. I tugged his shirt up and over his head. The warmth of his chest against mine brought such relief. I was unbuttoning his trousers. Relief, rescue. I stood up, I was naked; he stood up, he was naked. He sat back on the couch; I went back to where I'd been. I would like to say what followed was hurried, an accident, entirely about needs fulfillment and nothing more, but that wasn't the case. We were slow about it, without any awkwardness, without utterance, deliberate, tender. We were smiling. I remember thinking he'd been with other people, but he and I hadn't used condoms since we were young, so we didn't now. We shifted, we were prone, he was inside me. For the longest moment, he didn't move, I didn't move. In that stillness we were as close as two people can be. But it couldn't last: soon there was motion again, breathing, noise, and we were flying apart, very far apart. As I got dressed, I filled the space with chatter about my week

ahead, oh, my busy life. Ezra was quiet, politely solici-
tous. Then I left. And *that*, Detective, was that.

This had all happened once or twice before, early on
after we'd split up, but not in a long while. The next
day we didn't talk about what happened, then more days
passed. I should have called him, but then again he could
have called me. Then the weeks went by without contact, and he disappeared.

But how could he do that, simply vanish? How could
he do that to me?

I turned onto the coast road without realizing it at
first. I was burning up, for the first time in three months
allowing myself to be angry: Ezra had left me one more
time. I was done with this stranger game, and I was
done with him. He'd moved on, and as the detective had
prompted me, it was time at last I did, too.

On the long drive home I thought about how I would
make it through the holiday season by accepting every
invitation that came my way. In the winter I might start
studying a new language and travel to the country where
it was spoken. I might come home with a new cuisine.
How about a new boyfriend? There was so much I'd
held myself back from, but no longer, and imagine if I'd
only kept this promise to myself to go abroad, imagine
if I had left town. Then I myself would not have had to
disappear.

2

GRAY SKIES EVERY MORNING THAT DECEMBER MADE it difficult for me to get out of bed, but I pushed myself to go to yoga class before heading to my studio, where I was the last to leave at night. I diligently put together plans for the beach house renovation (existing ersatz colonial in front, serviceable glass-and-steel modern facing the ocean), and the partner with whom I worked most closely—this was Rick, the one with whom I'd carried on the flirtation years before—was vocally grateful about my doing my part to bring in revenue, and he also noted that we'd see other referrals now for similar work, good for the coffers, bad for the spirit, but so be it. Evenings and weekends I made soup and stews while listening to opera or jazz and tried not to drink too much wine. I reread classics in bed and usually fell asleep with the lamp on. I decided to repaint my house and purchased sample colors in small quantities, limiting myself to a soothing range from sage to mocha. I also took some clippers to the back slope and hacked at the overgrown brush, only a start but already bright floral sprays were emerging from the thicket. I told myself I could do this; I could furnish my life so that I might once again be comfortable in it. Yet nights remained difficult. At night my being split into two selves, my new industrious self and my old weary self who knew better, the latter regarding the former with skepticism: How long will you be able to keep up this routine? When I felt this old self was starting to get snide and judgmental about the new self, I went out to dinner. I was still alone, except with people around me.

This was how the first Friday of the New Year I ended up sitting at the bar at a neighborhood bistro, working my way through a plate of pasta à la norma and a glass of Chianti, chatting up the bartender about nothing in particular. Even though I was staring right at the mirror behind the bar and could see the waiters in long aprons sweeping about the candlelit room, I didn't notice a man take the open stool next to me, not until the bartender asked him what he wanted. Unlike me, the man was tall enough to sit on the stool with his shoes on the floor. A dense cosmos of freckles covered his arms, revealed by rolled-back sleeves. When he smiled hello, I noted the way his hair was impeccably parted, like a straight, flat road cut through a field of wheat.

"You play tennis," he said. Before I could say yes, but not recently or well, he added, "I mean professionally."

"Oh, heavens no," I said.

"I thought—"

"I wonder who you have me confused with. And aren't most pros tall?"

"Not always. You look familiar to me. I'm sorry."

"Don't be sorry, I'm flattered. A professional tennis player? That's a first."

He looked familiar to me, too, but I couldn't place him. He was balancing his jacket over his knee. I offered to hang it up on the hook next to me under the bar.

"But you, you must play tennis," I said. "You're tall."

"I do, but I can't serve to save my life. Or your life. No one's life will ever be saved by my serving."

I had no reason to like him right away, but I did. The bartender uncorked a bottle of the same Chianti I was drinking, and the man, who introduced himself as Carey, tasted and approved it.

"You're going to drink that whole bottle?" I asked.

"I certainly hope not," Carey said. "I drove. You'll help, right?"

"Smooth move," I said.

"So smooth. I've got all the smooth moves."

Of course I needed to be wary of handsome men buying me drinks, but when was the last time that happened?

"I should say I suspected you weren't a pro," he said,

"but I was having dinner over in the corner with my friend— Oh, she's gone, she left."

"Wait, you were on a date?" I asked. I hadn't noticed him when I'd come in.

"No, no. She's just a friend. Wow, that would be icky. I get rid of one date and then come over here to flirt with you—"

"Ah," I said. "You showed your hand."

He scrunched up his face: caught.

"You were about to withdraw the compliment that I looked like an athlete," I said.

"This isn't going well," Carey said.

"I'm flattered you came over to flirt with me, and I wouldn't mind another glass of wine, thank you."

"What I was going to say was that it was my friend who was wondering about you, and she said you looked like a professional tennis player."

So they were watching me, coming up with a story about me, which was what anyone would do when observing a woman dining alone; or were they playing the stranger game? Well, no, because if they were, he wouldn't be telling me about it.

"And what did you say to that?" I asked.

"I said…" He paused.

"Make it good."

"Artist," he said. "More specifically, a painter. Are you a painter?"

I had been sitting on the bar stool with my best posture, but I slumped briefly.

"Not for a long time," I said.

I wasn't in the mood to be coy or make him guess, so I told him about my work. He turned out to be a developer. The corporation he worked for had made its name replacing citrus groves with gated communities. What I called a house, he referred to as inventory. In a way, his whole career was pitched the opposite from mine. His chief ambition, he revealed, was to make enough money to buy a lake house somewhere remote and permanently decamp there with a lover.

I said, "I hate to disappoint you, but I'm a city person through and through."

"You'll come around," he said.

"Oh, you think?"

"Give me time," he said.

"Like how much time?"

Carey shrugged. "A half hour?"

I should have stopped drinking, but I kept going because drinking at the bar seemed to be the premise by which I could keep talking to him. The conversation wound back to my projects, about which he asked good questions and showed interest, which made it difficult for me to write him off as a political troglodyte. He did proceed to tell me about everything that was wrong with our city, and therefore why he wanted to abandon it, and I did want to say bye, nice knowing you. Although after a half hour of wine (no, more like an hour), the lake house scheme was beginning to appeal to me.

Every now and then the bartender asked me, "Still doing okay?"

I wondered what we looked like that brought out the chaperone in him. I glanced outside and noticed that it had started to rain finally. It was coming down hard.

"We need that," I said.

"We do," Carey said. "But too much all at once can be bad, too."

"Oh, dear," I said. "We're talking about the weather. It's come to that."

I noticed that he had a need to align the objects in front of him: the dessert card parallel with the edge of the bar; the dessert forks the bartender laid out so we could share a slice of chocolate cake parallel with each other; the empty wine bottle in longitude with his empty glass. He might be controlling, intense; his charm made me suspicious. But I was smitten. Also drunk. I almost reached over to his arm to play connect-the-dots with his freckles.

"So do you come here often?" I asked.

He chuckled. "I do indeed. What's a nice girl like you doing in a place like this?"

"No idea," I said. "What's your sign?"

"My sign is yield," he said. "And yours?"

I should have said it was stop.

"Want to drive me home?" I asked. I'd called a car

to get to the restaurant so I could drink and not worry about driving.

Carey signaled the bartender for the check, and when he looked back at me, I was even more smitten because he was rosy cheeked, boyish, like he very much wanted not to mess this up.

As I was handing him his jacket and putting on my own, he said, "By the way, I like your sweater."

He said this with his head cocked, one eyebrow arced, waiting for me to respond. I was wearing a lavender cashmere V-neck, and it looked fine on me but wasn't tight, not the sort of sweater to show off anything, the opposite. I wasn't sure how I should respond—with counterinnuendo, was that how this worked? I wanted what I wanted that night, I will freely admit it, but didn't know if I would be bold enough at the critical moment.

All I said was "Thanks, it's new."

Of course it was stupid to get in a car with him, both of us intoxicated. Thankfully we didn't have to drive far, and he parked in front of my house and came in. I gave him a tour, switching on lights as we went. He noticed the patches of sample paints and pointed at a color he liked.

"The lighter green would be better for resale," he said.

"I'm not thinking about selling."

"One should always be thinking about selling. Especially given that we're moving to the lake house."

"Good point. But at certain times of day, the lighter

green seems anemic to me. You need to see it in the morning," I said.

Yes, that was an invitation, and I knew what I was doing, showing him the main room, the kitchen first, saving the bedroom for last. I turned on two lamps. He turned off one. Was he modest? He had to bend down a little bit to kiss me. I discovered he was freckled everywhere when I unbuttoned his shirt and pulled it free from his trousers. Then we were on the bed and things picked up. I was too much in my head and tried to let go. He slipped off everything. He was even better looking naked. I was still mostly clothed, wearing my admired sweater, though he'd unzipped my pants. They were tight. And as he stood and tried to pull them off, they turned inside out and got caught on my ankles. He was too aggressive, dragging me down toward the foot of the bed, and my sweater bunched up around my chin. My butt was at the edge of the mattress; I almost fell off.

And in that moment, a turn. Carey managed to tug one pant leg off, but left the other inside out and cuffed around my ankle. There was nothing lovely about this, and when I pulled my sweater down so I could see him better, he looked neither soulful nor sexy. He swayed a bit. We'd had too much to drink, and I thought maybe we ought not to go any further, but he was moving forward now, eager, superhard, not the man I'd bantered with earlier—a wave of panic rose up from my stomach to my throat.

Farce seemed the quickest way out: I deliberately slipped off the bed onto the rug, oops. Carey remained standing, frowning, neither helping me up nor kneeling to be with me on the floor. He simply stood there. I watched his erection all but vanish. I wanted to cover myself up.

"Game over," he said. "You win. Or maybe I win. Does anyone actually win?"

I'd managed to get the pant leg over my foot and pulled my sweater down over my hips, and I was sitting on the bed again, pushing myself back. Now Carey was the one who sat down on the floor, naked, exposed.

"What do you mean does anyone actually win?" I asked.

"Your sweater," he said.

"What about it?"

"You didn't see me? You never saw me? Maybe then I do win."

I started shivering because suddenly I knew what he would tell me next.

"I was there when you bought it," he said.

I'd picked out this lavender V-neck that same day I'd followed the woman who tried on men's sweaters. I'd walked back across the department store to continue shopping for myself. This was a month ago.

"And you really never saw me?" he asked. "All this time, never?"

"Get out," I said.

Carey held up both hands, surrendering. "Like I said, game over—"

"You've been stalking me this whole time—"

"I wasn't *stalking* you," Carey said. He was standing again, stepping into his briefs. "I was playing—"

"Then why would you talk to me tonight? Those aren't the rules! How is this even the stranger game?"

"But that *is* how it's played," Carey said matter-of-factly.

I didn't know what he was talking about. "Get out," I said again.

"I'm sorry," he tried, but I was having none of it. I wanted him gone. "I really am," he said. "I screwed up."

"Get. Out."

He didn't explain himself or try to stay, and he also didn't look back at me when he let himself out, although he did apologize one last time. I jumped up the moment the door was shut and bolted it. I waited a good ten minutes after his car drove off to make sure he didn't return. I wanted to call the police, but to say what, to report what, the end of civilization? I thought about contacting Detective Martinez, but again, to what end? So she could admonish me for being so reckless?

I thought about all of the places I'd been in the last weeks and wondered when Carey had been watching me. The irony was acidic: I thought I was so expertly stealthy when I followed strangers, but most of that time, I'd been a subject, too. Although he couldn't have been trailing me the entire time because I certainly didn't spot anyone that rainy night when I got lost north of the city. He probably had learned enough about my routines to know where to find me whenever he wanted. He knew where my studio was and my yoga class and where I liked to hike and get takeout. It was likely that before coming home with me he already knew where I lived.

I scrubbed myself in the shower. I remade my bed with fresh linens. I refused to let this get to me, but I couldn't sleep and got dressed, went out to my car, backed out onto the street and made sure, extra sure no one was following me. It was three in the morning when I let myself into Ezra's cold apartment and crawled into his bed. He'd been gone four months, but his pillows smelled like him, like cinnamon. I cried. This was a very bad idea. I'd let the night defeat me, although I did eventually fall asleep.

FIFTEEN WAS EZRA'S FAVORITE NUMBER. IF HE RETIED his left sneaker, he had to retie his right, too. He wanted to put tomatoes in everything, but he didn't care for tomato soup. The cello was his favorite instrument. His favorite color was green, but brown greens, not blue greens, and definitely not yellow greens. He was left-handed and couldn't use a fountain pen because he'd smear the ink when he tried to write anything with it.

The novel he was writing was set in Paris, though the longest he'd lived there was for three months one summer during college before I knew him well. He had been to France two or three times before that. However, he said writing the novel kind of killed the place for him, and one reason he might never finish this book was because he'd fallen out of love with its setting. If anyone asked him what the novel was about, he'd say it was about people who had no desire to live where they were living but couldn't figure out how to leave. The working title was *Landlocked*.

Ezra got cold easily, and when we were together, rather than have a duvet on our bed, we'd come up with a system of layers of blankets so I could throw off some when I became too warm. I loved the parts of his body where he was ticklish, like the side of his chest; he was lean and I liked to run my fingers along the grooves between his ribs, and he'd learned to tolerate this, if not enjoy it a little.

He knew that my favorite number was forty-five, three times his favorite number (he always noted), and a long while ago he'd promised we'd go on a fantastic trip when I turned forty-five (not forty, not fifty). He knew I was fond of men's watches, and he bought me several over the years, calling himself my royal timekeeper. He knew I loved anything with mushrooms, and it was no accident he was ever perfecting his mushroom risotto, that this was what he was making when I saw him the last time. The guitar was my favorite instrument, and he tried (but failed) to learn it for me; I appreciated the effort. My favorite color was technically not a color, black, and this was a source of amusement for him; when we shopped together (which wasn't often), he pulled red and orange outfits off the rack for me as a challenge. I was right-handed and loved fountain pens, which he'd buy for me if ever he saw one that was onyx with gold trim——he spent too much money on fountain pens for me—and he'd buy me journals, too, although I was never a diarist.

Long ago when I was trying to be a painter, I was keen on portraiture, and even though Ezra thought no novel should come with a cover that had people on it because it was the reader's job to picture the characters an author invented, he said one of my portraits would be on his dust jacket. He said the book would be judged by its cover and therefore do well.

Because I was always warm and he ran cold, and even though we lived in a warm climate, during the winter when we went out, I'd wind a scarf around my neck, only to give it to Ezra, who sometimes was already wearing a scarf, and he'd walk around wearing both scarves like it was the height of fashion; I think he wanted to look a tad ridiculous to amuse me. I loved it when he kissed my neck, his always cool lips, the soft brush of his beard. I loved it when he stood behind me, simply stood there and held me, his arms a tight sash.

I never imagined I could know so much about another person and his body, nor he remember everything about me and mine. This sustained intimacy was what I missed most, our evolving lexicon, our constant conspiracy, his protection, the way I forever felt saved from what would have been a lonelier life. When I thought about meeting someone new, I was overwhelmed by how very long it would take to achieve the same closeness I'd known with Ezra, which was maybe why I hadn't really tried to meet anyone.

But then again there was apparently so much I didn't know about Ezra, and how could that be? Was there anything he didn't in turn know about me? No, nothing, or that's what it felt like, and I needed to dwell on this imbalance: it was significant.

When I woke up at Ezra's place, disoriented, then sadly remembering where I was and why, this was what I tried to focus on, Ezra the secret keeper, the man who could disappear without a trace. I was mad at myself. One horrible night with a creep had driven me back to Ezra, who was conveniently easy to fall in love with when he wasn't around.

And yet: Where was he?

I KEPT THE CURTAINS DRAWN IN THE FRONT OF THE house. Whenever I left, I scanned the street before I got in my car. At my morning yoga class, I unrolled my mat in the back corner, not to watch everyone else but so I could remain mostly unobserved. I cooked at home or ordered in. The only time I didn't move through the world extra-alert about who might be spying on me was when I went for a run around the reservoir because I needed to concentrate on my pace and not tripping, and even then I had to sprint to elude my paranoia, so fast sometimes that I couldn't make it through my usual five miles. This was why I wasn't able to ascend the final slope one morning and instead was breathing hard and walking past the dog park. I didn't recognize Detective Martinez out of uniform, a leash in each hand. Her two big wooly dogs didn't want her to stop to say hello to me. They were half her size and trying to tug her in opposite directions.

"Are you okay, Rebecca?"

Stopping to say hi made my heart race, and I had to bend over a moment.

"How have you been?" she asked.

I gave her a thumbs-up.

"I wish I had something new to tell you," she said.

"It's okay, Detective Martinez. You're off duty."

"Lisa," the detective said. "Hey, hey," she said to her dogs, pulling them toward her. "Sit, sit."

The dogs obeyed for all of ten seconds.

"They're handsome," I said.

"A handful, you mean. You want to hear something funny? They're rescue dogs, right. I figure there's some husky in there, some shepherd, a few other breeds. But I never really stopped to think what their parents looked like."

"I took your advice," I said.

"Oh?"

"I've been trying to move on."

"That's good to hear."

The detective could tell I wasn't happy about it. Even when she wasn't on the job, she stared at me without blinking.

"Something happened," I said, and right there on the sidewalk, me in my running kit and the detective trying to control her dogs, with other people jogging by and guiding their puppies into the dog park, I told her all about Carey and his revelation back at my house. Everything came out about the awful almost sex, how I ended up at Ezra's and how I was convinced now that everyone was playing the stranger game: the guys on the basketball court down the bend and the people driving by and all of the dog walkers, even the damned dogs probably.

The detective didn't respond at first. I waited to be scolded for bringing Carey home without knowing him, but instead she held both leashes with her right hand so she could squeeze my arm with her left.

"What a creep. That's awful," she said. "But listen, not everyone is like that. There are still people in the world you can trust."

I admit I did like hearing this.

"You know what bothers me the most?" I asked. "That the guy wasn't following the rules. I'm such a goody two-shoes. Of all things, that's what I can't let go of!"

"Oh, but that is the way people are playing now," Detective Martinez said. "For the thrills. They pick out random strangers like before, but now they see how long they can follow them—days, weeks. The endgame is exactly what happened to you. Contact, seduction, worse."

"Worse? Worse how?"

The detective did not elaborate. "At first, as you know, we were dealing with missing persons. Now it's all about the stalking, persistent stalking, sometimes criminal."

I rubbed my arms. I'd gotten cold. The detective couldn't keep her dogs from pulling her down the hill.

"Please be careful, Rebecca," she said. "And don't try to figure any of this out."

I DIDN'T LISTEN TO HER. I STARTED LEAVING WORK
early to go to the nearby mall, where I would ride the
escalator to the top floor and stand at the railing of the
atrium, peering down at the three floors of shops beneath, trying to identify anyone I thought might be a
player. What was I looking for? Anyone loitering alone,
standing off to the side, staring at people streaming by.
Someone who might make a sudden move and dart off
after a passerby. My plan was that if I spotted someone
whom I suspected might be inaugurating a follow, I
would sweep downstairs and follow the player as long as
I could, although this never worked because by the time
I reached the lower floor, I'd lost the player.

At the museum on long lunch breaks, I tried to do
the same thing, deciding the man in the untucked black
shirt and black jeans with tinted glasses wasn't looking at
the exhibit of color field paintings; he was in fact trail-

ing the woman with the jacket tied around her waist and two sets of glasses, the ones on a lanyard that she put on briefly to read the wall text, and the ones she let slip off her forehead onto the bridge of her nose to look at the art. Then it looked to me like the woman with two pairs of glasses herself may not have been truly studying the art or reading the wall text, and that this was all a ruse because she was following two teenagers in love, a boy and girl with equally narrow bodies and their arms coiled around each other. At least they couldn't be players; they were too preoccupied with each other to follow anyone.

But where did this end? Because in the mall, in the museum, I began to think that anyone and everyone could be playing the stranger game, and every follower him- or herself could be a subject in an infinite regression of pursuit.

I was thinking a lot about the broken rules, and sure, I could see how the first rule might fall away easily enough: followers might want to track subjects who intrigued them rather than those who at any given moment happened to pass by. I understood how according to Detective Martinez ignoring the second rule had become the norm, but I suspected that making contact wasn't merely an act of seduction; it was also the case that followers wanted to know if there was any truth in what they speculated about their subjects. However, breaking the third rule mystified me. What did it feel like to violate someone's privacy not once but repeatedly? Was there no hesitation in this, no shame?

One morning the second week in February, I was having trouble concentrating while working on a proposal for a new charter school and decided to ride the metro, something I hadn't done in a long while; riding trains always had a way of relaxing my mind. At one station, a man and a girl who could only be his daughter boarded and sat down across from me; they had the same pale complexion with faintly penciled-in eyes, the same small mouth and dot of a nose. He was wearing a suit; she was in a plaid school uniform. They sat very close to each other, didn't speak to one another, and each stared straight at me. Not in my direction, but at me, making eye contact. At first I looked away, and then when I turned back, they were still staring. I focused on the girl and stared back; she blinked. And that was that, they each withdrew a tablet from a bag and started scrolling through whatever they were reading. The girl got off the train first, the father two stations later. To school, to work—nothing unusual.

The next day I took the same train at the same time to catch the man and his daughter again. They appeared on the same schedule, wearing more or less the same outfits, exhibiting the same affect, but this time they took tandem seats at the other end of the car from me (the same middle car as the day before). Once again they stared at a woman sitting across from them, and like me, the woman looked away, looked back, and engaged. I couldn't tell, but I thought she was staring at the man, not the girl, and also this time it was the man who appeared to blink first. Once again the man and his daughter removed their tablets after losing the staring contest.

The next day, the same routine. Not with me, not with the woman from the day before (who wasn't on the train), but with a teen boy who took on the girl—and as far as I could tell, the boy blinked first. Were they even aware of what they were doing? They had to be, but their shtick was so deadpan, it was hard to say. Was this their own private version of the stranger game?

And then I wondered how many kinds of games people played with strangers every hour every day. We were, each of us, isolated creatures who ached for proximity, for intimacy with others, but who also out of primal self-preservation insisted on and maintained a safe distance. These stranger games we invented shuttled us somewhere halfway between stations of affinity and detachment, but more often than not we ended up at the latter destination. It was a miracle anyone ever connected with anyone. Most of the time we were cast back into our own longing.

I got off at the airport, the end of the line, and as often seemed the case these last months, I was going to be late for a meeting with my partners. I clicked a ride-hailing app on my phone. As was also the case recently, I was easily distracted, and when the car appeared, I'd forgotten to type in my office address.

When I got in, the driver said, "Say when, and I'll go."

This sounded odd. "Go?" I said.

And he pulled away from the curb.

"Oh, wait, I didn't say where," I said.

The driver pulled behind a black sedan and changed lanes again when it did.

"You don't say where. We just follow when you say go."

"I'm sorry, what?"

The driver slowed down and checked me out in his rearview mirror. He let the black sedan roar off ahead of us.

"My apologies," he said. "I thought you were playing. Where do you want me to take you?"

"You thought I was playing the stranger game."

We had exited the airport proper and were driving too slowly down a wide boulevard; the driver behind us honked.

"It's okay, you can tell me," I said.

"You didn't enter a destination," the driver said. "That usually means people want to play the game."

"And they say go and you follow whomever is in front of you."

The driver nodded.

"For as long as your passengers want," I said. "And then they pay the fare."

He nodded again.

"Is it mostly people coming into the airport who want to play?"

"Not always, but yes, lately, mostly from the airport," the driver said. "Tourists."

"I guess it's a good way to see the city?"

A fare was a fare to him, or maybe he liked the challenge: follow that car.

"So do you want to play, or do you have somewhere you need to be?" he asked.

I thought about seeing what a taxi-assisted follow might be like, but I said, "I have somewhere I need to be."

THEN ONE WEEK LATER THERE WAS THIS.

I was hiking an upper trail of the park canyon that bordered privately held land. There was a scattering of houses father down the ravine, but only one notable house up here, a never-occupied stucco hull wrecked on a sharp tor. A steep white wall made it next to impossible to peer in, but from where I was standing up top, right at the point where a secondary trail veered off, I could see the way the house stepped down the slope, a layer cake jostled during an earthquake. Some windows had been installed, many had not, and only part of the red tile roof was in place. The drop-off beyond the house was severe, likely making for a panoramic view from the broad terrace, which didn't appear to be finished as yet with any kind of parapet or rail. There were rumors about what might have happened: cost overruns due to real gold being used to trim imported marble; the accidental death of a child on the site; familicide. Most locals ignored the article that had run last year offering a more mundane explanation: the original owner had died ten years ago, and his aging widow still hoped to finish the project in tribute, although with every passing year that appeared less likely; her heirs would no doubt unload the property.

I was resting a moment and drinking from my water bottle when a bald man in a tracksuit rushed past me. He was pulling a woman behind him, a woman with wild eyes and a medusan fall of blond hair. He wasn't holding her hand so much as gripping her wrist. She was wearing a matching tracksuit. She blinked back at me in distress. Something untoward was happening. Instead of heading down the trail, they veered off onto the path leading up to the iron gate of the unfinished house, the gate weathered and warped enough to be pushed open just enough to enter. The couple shuffled down the front walk, the man still tugging the woman in tow, and they went around, but not as far as I could tell inside, the house, disappearing within the walled compound.

If that wasn't odd enough, a minute later another man and another woman hurried past me, too, and there was something about the way this second pair kept glancing around apprehensively that signaled they were players. They had to be: the woman held her forefinger over her mouth, be quiet, as they also wiggled through the gate and crept down the path to the house. Although unlike the first couple, these two went up to the front door, which (maybe not surprisingly) was unlocked. It opened with a creak even I could hear from a hundred yards up the hill. They went in, shutting the door behind them.

I half wanted to follow the followers and see how good they were at remaining undetected, and of course I was alarmed by the first couple in the tracksuits, but I was also wary of getting drawn in. I returned to the main trail and headed down the hill with the steep wall on my right; I continued around some rocks and down a ways, and then I thought I heard yelling coming from the abandoned house. I stopped. Silence. Then, yes: a bass voice shouting, a soprano in response.

I went back up the main trail and back down the side trail, this time all the way to the gate, which I now shimmied through, too. The shouting became clearer.

Him: "Don't you."

Her: "Stop it."

I took out my phone and pressed 911 without completing the call. The creak of the front door announced my entry, and I had to wait what seemed a dangerous amount of time for my eyes to adjust to the dim dusty interior.

Him: "You told me you were through with all that."

Her: "I said, let go."

Him: "I trusted you. You swore it."

I followed a corridor toward daylight. There were bedroom-sized rooms off the corridor, and spaces probably meant to be finished as bathrooms.

Her: "Why are you doing this? You stay there. You stay right there."

Was this the first couple or the second, or some combination of the two? I assumed it was the couple in the tracksuits. I couldn't see anyone yet, but then I emerged on a landing where more light streamed through opaque windows. I came up to a railing where I could look down on a grand space below. Off to one side was a stone fireplace; the second couple, the players, were crouching down on the other side of the room, whispering to each other. I still couldn't see where the shouting tracksuit couple was, maybe outside on the terrace.

Him: "Where are you going? Come here."

Her: "I said stay there."

The woman was in trouble, and if I screamed (and called 911 at the same time), it would disrupt whatever malevolence was unfolding. And this made me ask why the crouching couple didn't themselves make their presence known. Oh, right, because they were playing the stranger game, so of course they weren't going to take action (if they were playing by the original rules, which it would appear they were).

But I was wrong about that.

Right as I was about to scream "Hey" as loud as I could and as many times as was necessary, the man player stood up, very much revealed himself by flailing his arms, and shot outside to the terrace through an opening where a sliding glass door could go, and out of view.

His companion yelled, "What are you doing?" And: "Careful!"

The first shouting man: "What the."

The man player, in a reedy voice: "You leave her alone, okay? Back off and leave her alone."

The first man: "Hey, buddy, mind your own—"

The man player: "Why don't you get lost?"

The woman player: "Should I call the police? Don't touch him. Stop."

The first man: "Motherfucker."

The man player: "All right, all right, why don't we all calm down here?"

Then I heard some shuffling and muffled screaming and un-muffled screaming (from the woman player), and I was fairly sure that someone was being wrestled to the ground. I tapped the call button on my phone, only to discover I had no reception.

However, as I was trying to make the call, the bald man in the tracksuit appeared inside the house. The woman player took two steps back. And the man stomped across the main room and out a side door. I wasn't sure what was happening. I looked at the windows to my left and saw the man in the tracksuit run up an exterior flight of stairs, past the upper level where I was standing. I heard him at the gate.

Meanwhile the woman in the tracksuit had come into the main room and was with both players, thanking them repeatedly.

The woman player asked, "Are you okay?"

The woman in the tracksuit said, "I will be. He wasn't always this way. But oh, oh…" She squeezed the arm of the man player and said, "Thank you. You saved me, you really did."

Soon the three of them were outside and going up the exterior stairs, leaving me alone in the abandoned house. After I heard them go through the gate, I left, too, and by the time I reached the trail, all four of them had vanished.

Where had the stranger game players started following the tracksuit couple? How far had they pursued them? And *what* had I just observed? Was I delirious?

I hiked the main trail down past two tiers of tennis courts toward the parking lot. My water bottle was empty, so I made a detour to the drinking fountain by the restrooms. The fountain was outside the men's room side of the building, the entry to the men's room behind a wooden fence. I heard two voices.

The first I recognized as the reedy voice of the man player who had saved the day: "That was awesome."

The other belonged to the bald man in the tracksuit: "Glad you liked it."

"No, it was amazing. So how much do I still owe you?"

"Three hundred should do it."

"Right. Here you go."

I walked away quickly toward the parking lot. I looked

over my shoulder and saw the man player behind me, not the man in the tracksuit. I got in my car first and watched the player slip into an expensive coupe across the lot. His companion in the passenger seat was beaming at him. They sped off. It was a full five minutes before the bald man in the tracksuit appeared in the parking lot, too, and climbed into an SUV; its driver was the woman with the tracksuit, except she'd lost the voluminous wig, revealing a tight brunette ponytail—meaning what?

Meaning this whole game had been staged for a fee.

I couldn't add it up. Was the non-tracksuit couple truly playing the stranger game? Was the scenario set up so the man player could emerge the hero and impress the woman player? How had this been arranged? And at the end of the day, what did the woman player know? Did she figure out the scheme? No, the man player had been thrilled with the way everything unfolded. The woman would remain in the dark. To her friends, she would boast about the man's unhesitating valor.

I was in such a fog that when I pulled into my driveway, I didn't notice at first the man sitting by my front door, holding a cone of bright flowers. It was Carey.

I SAT IN MY CAR AWHILE CONTEMPLATING MY OPTIONS. I could pull back out of the driveway and zoom off. To make matters worse, a home alarm somewhere nearby started blaring, filling the neighborhood for several minutes with a fast-repeating siren. When the alarm was turned off and I finally got out of my car and approached him, Carey held out the flowers for me. I stared at them without accepting them. He drew them back to his chest, and then he sneezed.

"Slightly allergic," he said and extended the bouquet once again, a dozen velvety roses, open, honeyed.

I took them from him.

"That wasn't me," he said. "I got lost in that idiotic game. And I was drunk. And then, I don't know. I only thought I'd talk to you. I never expected to end up here. I know I'm terrible, and there's nothing I can say, except I was not myself—or I wasn't who I want to be. And the

worst part of it is you told me, you told me very explic-
itly how you'd not really been out with anyone since…
I am so sorry."

When he was done I finally looked at him: his eyes
were like ponds, two perfect blue ponds. I hated myself
for being as attracted to him as much as I was, even now,
this freckled monster.

"Is Carey your real name?"

"It is," he said and sounded hopeful: that I was asking
this question meant I might forgive him.

"Thank you for the flowers," I said. "Apology accepted."

I was eternally lonely. I wanted to ask him in and make
tea and laugh off what had happened. What a world,
what a dark age we lived in—why were we doing this to
one another? I craved banter. And touch. I suspected he
might actually be one of the good guys but had strayed.
Wasn't I a great believer in second chances?

I said, "I was on a hike. I need to go inside now and
clean up."

"Of course," Carey said and stepped away from the
door, switching positions with me, backing down the
front walk.

When I didn't know what to say, I often resorted to
expressions I never used. I said, "Bye now," and I said,
"Ciao," my head already buzzing with regret.

I MOVED THROUGH MY DAYS AT A SLOWER TEMPO. I showed up where I was expected, met deadlines, and even managed to get my bedroom repainted a color that rightly should have been called weak tea. However, the time between appointments and driving from place to place, lying in bed at night, in the morning—this time seemed endless to me. Ezra had been gone six months, there was that. I'd moved his possessions to a nearby storage facility, not that he had much, because it would have been too costly to pay the insurance; I sold his car for not very much money, which I used for the storage. And then also I had nothing to look forward to—not only nothing to look forward to, but also no memory of having had anything to look forward to for a long while.

A memory from when I was four: our house was a block away from an elementary school, and one early fall morning I was sitting under a tree by the end of the drive-

way, playing with the fallen pods and leaves in the dirt.
Some teenage girls walked by on their way to school and
thought I was cute, and they stopped to say hi to me. And
it occurred to me in that moment that the only things
that existed in the world were what I could observe: the
pods, the leaves, the dirt, the tree. The tricycle I'd abandoned up the driveway, the driveway. The girls with their
hair falling in their faces as they bent down to talk to me,
their backpacks, their sweaters with knobby knitting, their
denim skirts, their legs, their sandals. What I could not
see did not exist (like my mother's god). I say I had these
thoughts that morning when I was four, true, but naturally my ability to articulate them only came years later,
and Ezra was one of the first people I met who didn't
think I was strange to have had this epiphany so young;
the opposite. He said, Me, too.

It was odd to think about how coincidence worked
in the life of an atheist. For the believer, when something uncanny happened, it could be read as part of a
plan; there was always an explanation. For someone like
me, coincidence might be delightful (or unsettling), but
there never was any greater scheme to consider. But then
at the same time, we atheists potentially became blind
to hidden plots; we didn't perceive patterns; encounters
that appeared accidental might not be accidental at all.

Two weeks after Carey showed up with flowers, I
spotted him at the museum at noon (and I knew I hadn't
mentioned that I liked to come here during lunchtime,

but it was likely he'd followed me in at some point). I stood at the top of the steps leading down into the sunken sculpture garden behind the original building; because it was on the opposite side of the museum from newer and more popular pavilions, the garden was less visited. Carey couldn't have been more than fifty feet away. I pulled back behind a palm tree. His back was to me; he didn't turn around. He was sitting on a bench, drinking coffee, staring at a set of brushed steel cubes arranged to evoke a dancing man. He shifted on the bench to face the red-painted steelwork that resembled a giant tricorn hat tipped onto its side. He was facing the sculpture, but his gaze appeared fixed on nothing in particular. He was slouching a bit, and he seemed a little rumpled to me, his shirt untucked, his hair tousled.

When he stood, I hopped around the corner into a gift shop. I waited. Carey walked past the shop out to the street. I waited another moment, then followed him. He was headed in the same direction as my studio, and I was paranoid enough to think he was looking for me again. But he walked two blocks beyond my building to another, grander one with a fountain flowering in front. I'd forgotten he'd mentioned how close his office was to mine. I watched him go inside: there was something defeated about his rounded shoulders, something pressing against him, an unseen weight.

I had no reason to believe he'd emerge from the building at the end of the day because he could have gone out for a meeting or to do who knew what at any time, but I parked halfway down the block from the rear parking garage anyway, hoping to catch him when he emerged. I waited an hour, and voilà. We were on a one-way street, and I was able to scoot in two cars behind him.

Rush-hour traffic I'd learned was perfect for the stranger game; you had the screen of the cars in front of you, and everyone moved along slowly enough to make trailing another car easy. Carey wove his way up to a main boulevard and headed east, veering off two miles later into the parking lot of an organic grocer. I knew if I went inside the store, too, I might expose myself, him coming up the aisle I was sneaking down. But that didn't happen. I saw him first and was able to take cover behind a pyramid of apples. He was standing in front of a refrigerated case of prepared foods, selecting plastic containers and scrutinizing the ingredients.

I wanted to slide in next to him and give him a start. What I really wanted to do was invite him over and cook him dinner so he didn't have to eat the oversalted junk he was collecting in his cart. When he turned in my direction, I left the store, and I drove off before he came out.

This happened on a Thursday, and I thought about trying to track him again the next day, maybe all the way back to where he lived, but I didn't. I'd spent too much time at night imagining what he might be doing, maybe going to bed early like me because it was easier to sleep than to wade through hours of nocturnal solitude.

I knew then that I'd see him again, although I didn't expect it would be so soon.

Saturday late afternoon I decided to go on my usual hike up in the park, leaving my car by the tennis courts and then walking up to the trailhead. When I passed the upper tier of courts, I spotted Carey on the farthest one from the path. There were no players on the three other courts, and Carey was by himself. He'd placed a wire basket of old balls by the baseline and was practicing his serve, the weak part of his game, which didn't look too weak to me. He tossed the ball high, very high, and he bore down on it hard like a windmill catching a sudden gust. He aced an invisible opponent on the deuce side, and then did the same on the ad.

When I thought he might be looking my way between serves, I waved hello. He let his racket fall to his side. We shouted hi at the same time.

"My buddy canceled on me last minute, but I'd already reserved the court," he explained.

"You serve incredibly well," I said from the other side of the fence. I'd walked over to his court but not through the gate. "You were being modest."

"I really wasn't," he said and decided to show me.

He bounced a ball a few times then tossed it toward the sun, arced his back and swung down at the ball. Down the line, perfect.

"It's a whole lot easier when you don't have an opponent," he said.

I liked the way his body looked when he served another ball, not like a machine, not like a windmill at
all, but graceful, an upright swimmer in full stroke out
of water.

"I have a backup racket," he said. "Do you want to play?"

"It's been so long," I said. "I'll be terrible."

"Oh, come on. It will be fun. Please?"

Suddenly I was on the opposite side of the court from
him swatting at balls and sending them sailing beyond
the baseline, twice over the fence, shrieking my apologies, my I-told-you-so's.

"Your form is coming back," Carey insisted.

"What form?" I said.

But he was right. The longer we rallied, the surer my
forehand. After a half hour, I was striking the ball cleanly,
with force, hitting it deep. We rallied for a long time,
and while I fancied myself fit, I found myself breathing
hard. We sat on the bench. I had to admit that this was
satisfying, finding my old rhythm.

"But it can't be fun for you," I said. "You're hitting
soft, I'm sure."

"I'm not! Honest. Want to hit some more?"

I trotted over to the other side, which had some shade
and which meant I didn't have to stare into the setting
sun when I tried to serve. We played points. We would've
kept going but soon would lose the light; these courts
weren't set up for night play.

"That was really fun," Carey said.

"It was. Would you like to go on a date with me?" I asked.

I probably looked as surprised as he did.

"A proper date," I added.

He blinked at me in disbelief and nodded quickly.

"You probably have plans for tonight," I said.

"Not anymore," he said.

"Now, wait. Don't go canceling on some other girl—"

"I was only going to hang out with the same tennis buddy who didn't show up today, him and his silly friends. Trust me, they won't miss me."

"That all sounds very guy-ish," I said.

"Very guy-ish. Grrr. You were saying?"

"Dinner, dancing, something like that," I said. "Maybe without the dancing."

Two hours later he picked me up and we were sitting out under a heat lamp on the back patio of my second-favorite neighborhood restaurant, not the one where we'd met. Carey was wearing a crisp white shirt, a trim blazer.

"I want to hear more about your work," he said. "How'd you get into it anyway?"

I ended up talking about myself all through dinner, answering Carey's questions, although my deliberate choice to leave Ezra out of my monologue was noticeable to me. When for instance I described a meaningful formative train trip through Europe looking at neoclassical architecture, I didn't mention that I'd traveled with Ezra.

"And you? You always wanted to be a developer?" I asked.

Carey laughed and said, "I wanted to be an artist," and at first I thought he was making fun of me. He wasn't. "I had no talent."

"Like you're no good at tennis?"

"I will admit I'm okay at tennis," he said. "Anyway, I interned for a real estate agent one summer, a family friend. One thing led to another, and I had my license, and there was a boom, I was off. But it's not like I chose this career—it happened to me. Business has been pretty rough lately though, so we'll see what happens next. We should change the subject. You're much more interesting than I am."

He seemed down. I tried to pour him another glass of wine—he'd had a glass and a half—but he said the rest of the bottle was mine. It was obvious he was trying to chart a different course for us than the last time.

He pulled up to my house to drop me off and said that the whole day had been unexpected and wonderful. I suggested he come in.

"This is a proper date," he reminded me.

"I'm having an unexpectedly wonderful time, too," I said. "I don't want it to end."

He hesitated but leaned toward me to offer me a gentle kiss.

We stood out on my terrace and looked at the city. When it became too cold, we went inside. We were moving into the kind of conversation that might make one vulnerable: I spoke openly now about the ups and downs of life with Ezra. He talked about his family, his parents' alcoholism, the older brother whom he'd revered and lost to addiction. When we were making out, he was the one who pulled back and said he should leave. I didn't want him to leave. He kept asking me if I was sure. How could I let him know I'd forgiven him and that, yes, I was sure?

I loved running my hand all the way from his freckled clavicle over his freckled chest down to his (less) freckled abdomen. He was shy at first. I suspected this was the real him he'd referred to, not the drunk guy playing me. But finally he began to explore my body with a confident hand. Before we fell asleep he thanked me for giving him a second chance, but in my heart I felt somehow like it was the other way around, that he was the one allowing me back in a second time.

When I woke up in the morning, facing the wall with my back to him, I was certain I was alone and that he'd crept off in the middle of the night. I couldn't feel his heat, his weight on the bed, and I rolled over quickly. But there he was, at once far away in sleep and close, here with me. What complete joy. I plotted our Sunday.

WE WENT TO THE FARMERS' MARKET AND RETURNED
to my kitchen with zucchini and mushrooms and pars-
nips and thyme. Carey turned out to be a fast chopper.
We made a frittata. Later we retreated to the bedroom,
slipping beneath blankets when the afternoon became
cool and we didn't want to shut the windows. This had
been an epic date and I didn't want Carey to go, although
he did, and I worried all night he'd disappear on me.
My anxiety was for naught; he came over the following evening and spent the night again. Same the night
after that, and the night after that. The weeks uncoiled
rapidly. Carey and I spent all our time in my house on
the hill, now huddled in bed, now moving about the
garden. Watching Carey take charge of my sorry plants
naturally made me think of Ezra and his botanic savvy,
and a part of me wished Carey and I were playing house
somewhere new, but when I thought about Ezra, I had

perspective now, and I could only hope that wherever he was, he had achieved the same contentedness.

During the week we trotted off to our respective offices, and although most people I had known in real estate worked evenings and weekends, Carey made time for me. He was between homes, as he put it, renting a studio somewhere he said was so provisional that he'd be embarrassed to show it to me; I didn't care one way or another, and so I never saw where he lived.

We didn't go out into the city much, although we discussed heading to the museum to see the retrospective of a minimalist painter we both liked, and to the new neighborhood sushi counter, and to the rehabilitated riverside park; we talked about going but never did. I did not introduce Carey to my few friends; I did not show him past or current projects. He did not talk about his work, and as far as I could tell, he was as alone in the world as I was. I knew better than to ask him to give up his temporary housing and move in with me, it was too soon, but I did ponder when in the near future I might propose it. Even so, he began to care for my home as if it were his. He rehung a closet door that with settling wasn't closing completely; he built the shelves I'd been wanting to put in my pantry; together we started in on repainting the exterior stucco.

One April afternoon I left him patching the wall in back while I made a run down to the hardware store. I was in the paint supplies aisle sorting through brushes, rollers, and whatnot when I could have sworn someone was watching me. I turned toward the end of the aisle: no one. But I had such a funny feeling about this that I stepped around to the next aisle, and there was Detective Martinez, out of uniform like the last time I'd seen her, pricing dimmer switches.

"Oh, hi," she said.

"Did you—? Were you—?"

No blinking.

"Hi," I said. "Weekend project?"

"Always. It never ends," the detective said. "How have you been, Rebecca?"

"Wonderful," I said, and her eyes widened: do tell. I didn't mention that Carey was the same guy I'd told her about before.

"What's his name?" Detective Martinez asked, and I revealed that much, and to be polite I asked about her own life, not expecting her to be forthcoming.

But she said, "My ex and I reconciled. And it's been great, actually."

"Wow," I said. "Love all around."

"Sounds like it."

"Well," I said.

"Right," she said. "I should get home with a light switch."

I headed back to the paint supplies aisle.

"Rebecca," the detective said. "I don't know if I should bring this up…"

My heart thudded.

"I'm assuming you've seen the same bank statement we did. Ezra's account."

I hadn't been paying attention to it because there was almost no money in the account, and in order for me to access the information, I had to go to the bank in person— honestly, I'd forgotten about it.

"He closed it out two months ago. We haven't been tracking it closely. We haven't been working the case much, but you knew that."

"He was here? He closed it out in person?"

"No. The money was wired to another account, a different bank—"

"Where?"

The detective shrugged. "We'd need an order to find that out," she said. "There's nothing criminal we can investigate. There's nothing that signals he's in harm's way, nothing we can act on. It's not like his landlord wants to evict him since you moved out his things…"

I had no reason to believe she wasn't telling me the truth, but I was pretty sure in fact she did know where Ezra was and either wasn't permitted or didn't think it prudent to tell me.

"I see. Did you close the case?"

The detective didn't answer my question, but she said, "This means he's alive. At least you can rest easy knowing that."

I could, I would, yes. But he didn't want me in his life, and that was cruel. I sighed so deeply that both the hardware store employee mixing paints and his customer stared at me. The detective looked at me with concern.

"You know what? It's okay," I said. "I'm with someone great, I'm happy. But thank you for telling me."

I wished she hadn't. Instead of driving directly home, I went to the storage facility. I borrowed a dolly from the manager and took the elevator to the top floor and found the numbered closet. Light from the hallway lit up the stack of book boxes: not much. I could probably get them all downstairs to the Dumpster in two or three trips.

I slumped down in the hallway and sat on the floor. I was not going to get rid of anything. I couldn't, not yet. Two thoughts at once: how much I hated Ezra, that selfish betrayer, and how much I missed him.

When I got home, Carey said, "You were gone a long time. I got worried."

I buried my face against his chest.

"You've been crying," he said.

I lied to him for the first time. It was such an unnecessarily elaborate story, too. Driving to the hardware store, I'd had to swerve to avoid these stupid boys on their skateboards, but one teenage girl driving behind me also swerved and hit an easement tree, causing the sapling myrtle to snap and fall on the hood of her car and shatter her windshield. The safety glass stayed in place; her airbags deployed. She was fine, shaken up but fine, and I'd helped her call the police (the boys ran off) and contact her mother, and I'd waited for her to get there.

Carey held me tightly and told me everyone was safe. I'd helped; I'd been a good person. We would return to our weekend now. Everyone was safe, he said again, and because I wanted to, I believed him. But the lie I told had cracked my new life open just enough for skepticism to seep in—doubt, suspicion, the old familiar dread.

FRIDAY NIGHTS WE TURNED OFF MOST OF THE LIGHTS in the house and sat close to each other in the dark, the two of us facing the city, the vista like a long film we were never done watching. Our conversations were never linear: we would digress and then have trouble winding our way back to whatever we'd initially been talking about. Sometimes we gave up. So I don't remember how we arrived here.

I asked, "How did you start playing the stranger game anyway?"

I found it peculiar that this never came up. We never discussed the way we'd met and what happened that first night. Carey had been contrite, I had forgiven him.

He took a moment to respond. "I'm never going to be able to make that up to you—"

"No, no, no," I said. "I'm not looking for any more apologies. I'm only curious how you got—"

"Hooked? A guy in my office was missing a lot of meetings with contractors. Someone told me what was going on, and at first I didn't know what this game was."

"It's ironic it brought us together," I said. "Do you think there are other stranger game couples out there?"

"Oh, I hope not. I mean…"

I chuckled. "I know what you mean."

And I thought that was that, except it wasn't.

I said, "The last time I myself was playing—"

"What? Hold on. The last time you were what?"

Carey pulled away from me. He switched on a lamp. He was frowning.

"You never said you played, too," he said.

He knew about what I believed Ezra had been up to, but not about my own forays.

"Wow," he said. "It's weird you never mentioned it."

"I know. I should have told you. Are you mad?"

He shook his head no. "How often did you play?"

And here again another lie. "Once or twice," I said. "A few times."

"To understand what Ezra might be experiencing?"

"Exactly. Do you want to hear about it? It's not that interesting."

"No, I don't need to know," he said. "You weren't in as deep as I was."

"I always followed the original rules. For the most part," I said.

"It starts with for the most part."

I described the driver who had picked me up at the airport thinking I was a tourist player, and then I told him about the scene I'd witnessed at the abandoned house and what I'd overheard by the men's room.

"Wow," Carey said again. "I heard about this but never saw it myself."

"Heard about what? This is a thing?"

"It's apparently become a thing. There's a whole network now of followers and stagers—"

"Stagers?"

"That's what they're called. You can hire them to do whatever you want within reason, and then you can entertain your fellow followers, who don't know it's all a show."

"Or you can impress someone by playing the hero."

"Like I said, I've never seen it, but it sure sounds like you did," Carey said and switched off the lamp, returning us to darkness.

"None of this resembles what Craig originally wrote about," I said. "I wonder if he's out there, if he knows what kind of madness he inspired."

"He must, don't you think?"

"I'm not sure. Wouldn't he have spoken out by now and made some sort of comment?"

"We don't know very much about him," Carey said. "Or I don't anyway. I shouldn't admit this, but I never read the article. Should I?"

"Don't bother now."

I was relieved Carey wasn't upset at me for not being
forthright, but I also wondered why he wasn't more bothered. During the weeks he was following me, he must
have witnessed me playing the game—did he realize that
now? I didn't ask. I didn't want to revisit the topic ever
again. However, I'd brought up the stranger game—I
was the one who reintroduced it into our lives.

The next day we went to the grocery store. Carey
wanted to celebrate the new season by making pasta
primavera, and while he was gathering asparagus and
string beans and peas, et cetera, I found myself watching
a woman hovering over the bin of avocados, squeezing
every one several times. I understood she wanted avocados that were ripe (or not yet ripe), but once she found a
few she approved of, why couldn't she move on?

"Check her out," I whispered to Carey.

"Finicky," Carey said.

After the woman selected an avocado and pushed her
cart out of produce and into dairy, I followed her—or
I should say we followed her, since Carey led the way.
Standing in front of a refrigerator case, the woman pro-
ceeded to pick up and sniff every quart-sized carton of
nonfat milk.

"You can't tell if it's good by smelling a closed carton,
can you?" I asked.

"I don't know," Carey said. "I hope she doesn't do this
now with the—"

Before he could finish his sentence, the woman was

opening every carton of large brown eggs. She wasn't going to stop at a carton with no broken ones; she had to survey every egg.

"I sort of get it," Carey said.

"You do?"

"She has a need for order. I do, too. She's hypercautious."

I thought about the way he liked to make sure his fork was parallel to his knife before he began eating. He liked towels to hang evenly on a bathroom rack. He was a bit compulsive.

"But with her," he said, "this is all because of some childhood accident involving—what?"

"Kayaks," I said. "At summer camp."

"Oh, I see. All of the boats looked the same, the dozen lined up for the kids to take out on the lake."

"Right. Actually it wasn't a lake, it was the ocean."

"Rough weather that day?"

"Yes. She had her hand on one bright yellow kayak, but some bossy girl pushed in front of her," I said, "and took it for herself, leaving the woman—the woman as a girl, I mean—an ugly, brown, banged-up kayak instead."

We had followed the woman from the dairy section down an aisle of canned vegetables and meats. She was examining tins of imported sardines.

"But then the scariest thing happened," Carey said.

We'd come too close to the woman and had to pretend to discuss which brand of whole tomatoes we preferred.

"The bright yellow kayak turned out not to be sea-worthy," I said. "There was a leak."

"It took on water fast."

"The girl in the bright yellow kayak was waving her oar around, panicking, sinking—and she hadn't fastened her life vest tightly enough, it was coming undone, bobbing up around her chin—"

"She was screaming," Carey said. "No one helping her."

"She didn't drown."

"Counselors saved her?"

"Yes, thankfully. But ever since then…" I nodded in the direction of the woman who was bent over a display of whole-bean coffee at the end of the aisle.

"It could have been her. She almost took the bright yellow kayak for herself simply because it was the prettiest."

"The prettiest isn't always the safest though."

"Best to inspect everything twice. Know what you've got," Carey said.

We grinned at each other, satisfied with ourselves, and finished our shopping. We lost track of the woman in the store, but then we saw her in front of us as we were exiting the parking lot. I was driving. When the woman slipped into the left turn lane, I did as well, which meant heading the opposite direction from my house. I didn't have to look over at Carey to know he approved.

The woman made a right; I stayed with her. She made

another quick right and headed up a steep incline into the hills overlooking the reservoir.

"You're good at this," Carey said.

"Better than you?"

He didn't answer me. Instead he said, "She'd like to be in a relationship, but she can't. She won't compromise, or she doesn't know how to."

"She needs the pots and pans arranged just so?"

"More that she has systems. If you finish two sticks of butter in a box of four, you're supposed to write down you need more on the grocery list."

"You can't wait until you run out and then put it on the list?"

"Certainly not," Carey said. "No one understands how important this is to her."

Following someone around the narrow bends of a hill road was tricky. In order not to get too close, I had to let the woman pursue an entire curve and trust she'd still be there when we drove the curve, too. It would seem she lived at the crest.

"She did fall in love once," Carey said.

"Only once? What happened?"

The woman had come to a stop in front of a rusty gate. It wasn't automated or the remote was broken; she had to get out of the car and slide it open manually. We were down the grade a ways, and by the time we made it to the top, the woman had driven through and closed the gate behind her. We didn't have a good view of her house. We could see the rain-stained metal fascia running around the eaves of what looked to be a modern box, but that was it. We could only imagine her view of the city on the other side, even more proprietary than mine.

"He died," Carey said. "Her one true love."

I winced at that. There was no one with whom she could share the best of all possible avocados. Carey sighed, too. We'd made ourselves sad, and that melancholy seemed to follow us home. We were unpacking our groceries in silence when Carey took the asparagus from my hand and set it on the counter. He pulled me into a hug, and we stood like that awhile, comforting each other with the tacit acknowledgment that at least we weren't alone.

Something was shifting. How to describe it? That night we embraced the way we usually did as we started to fall asleep, except we didn't eventually migrate to our separate sides of the bed, and I was surprised when I awoke at three in the morning to find us still entwined. This was a new need—authentic, urgent—and I liked it; I wanted more.

The next afternoon we were on the way to the movies when Carey, driving now, pointed out a minivan a few cars in front of us, the minivan packed with teenage girls in pink satin gowns. The driver was a guy in a tux, not much older.

"Where are they headed? A wedding?" I asked.

"A quinceañera," Carey said, and he glanced over at me in the passenger seat: Should we?

We followed the minivan to the park, to a fountain popular with event photographers. The teenagers filed out of the minivan and joined others already fanning out around the girl of the hour, all in white. We weren't so much focused on them, however, as much as the driver, who didn't get out from behind the wheel. He smoked two cigarettes in a row.

"What's his deal?" Carey asked. "He's the older brother chaperone?"

"I'm not sure," I said. "His mind is elsewhere."

The driver abruptly pulled out in Reverse and then drove away from the fountain and out of the park. I speculated that he probably had to collect another group of celebrants and bring them up here, but Carey disagreed. We followed him a mile or two down the road, and then he turned back into the park through a different entrance. This road wound past a onetime Western movie set turned into a playground, a miniature golf course, and then up into the hills. I thought Carey was getting too close to the minivan, so we dropped back, and when we found the driver again, he'd pulled into a small lot by a lookout point. There was the panoramic view, yes, but more immediately below, a clear shot of the fountain in the park where everyone was having photos taken with the birthday girl. The man sat on a bench and withdrew another cigarette from the breast pocket of his tux. He looked back at us sitting in Carey's car with the motor running—our cover was blown—but the man didn't seem to care and peered down again at the girls around the fountain.

We couldn't agree on what he was up to. I thought he was being creepy, spying on a young girl it would have been inappropriate to stare at close-up. Carey was convinced the man had recently lost someone—a sister—and he was simply too sad to stick around for the festivities. Twice now Carey's narratives for the strangers we followed arrived at loss.

We had missed our movie but didn't go to another screening. Out of the park, we were heading west.

Carey said, "Say when."

A pickup truck loaded with lawn mowers and rakes and coils of hoses drifted by. There were two women in the cab.

"When," I said.

It was a Sunday, not when I would have expected to find gardeners working, and I was used to seeing men in these trucks, not women. The boulevard took us through a series of commercial strips and then a pricier part of town with old mansions set back from the road and newer ones occupying the entirety of smaller lots. Carey thought the gardeners would turn off into one of these estates, but they didn't; they kept going, on through the next neighborhood. The road dropped down toward the ocean eventually, ten-plus miles from where we'd picked them up. They made a U-turn on the coast road to park on the beach side. The sun would set soon. There were no other cars parked nearby, and there wasn't official access to the beach here, but that was where the two women headed, leaving the pickup with all its gear exposed to highway thieves. One woman wore a backpack.

By the time we shot ahead several hundred yards and made a U-turn ourselves, the women had stepped over the guard rail and were climbing down the rocks toward the narrow stretch of sand.

"They're going to take a walk and watch the sun set?" I asked.

Carey didn't think so. "They're here on a mission. What's in the backpack?"

We didn't go down the rocks after them, but we could watch them from the road. When one looked back our way, we both ducked behind Carey's car. She stared at the car for a long moment and said something to the other woman. They were the same height, had the same long hair—each wore a gold bracelet reflecting the dying sun. They must have decided we weren't a threat, and they headed a little ways down the beach. They removed a box from the backpack.

"There's been a recent death," Carey said. "A brother, a husband—"

"Carey," I said. "This is always where you go, to such a dark place…"

But I had to be quiet because he was right: from the

box, one woman removed a plastic bag, into which the other dug her hand and withdrew a fistful of cinders, which she flung into the approaching tide. They were spreading someone's ashes. The second woman took a turn. The first woman again. And then the second dumped the rest of the cremains in the ocean foam. We decided to head off before they climbed back up the rocks.

"I don't know," Carey said back at my place, on the couch, the lights off, the city flickering with extra life. "I feel like it's everywhere you turn."

"Death?"

"Loss in general."

I had decided to ask as gently as I could if this pervasive grief he experienced had a source. Were there losses in his own life he hadn't told me about?

"Can I be completely candid?" he asked. "You already dealt with one lost soul when you were with Ezra. You don't need another one with me."

I wasn't expecting this. There was something sweetly considerate about his thinking, even if he was off. I didn't think he was a perro perdido (nor was that necessarily how I would characterize Ezra). Although even as I told him this, I was asking myself if I was (why I was) possibly attracted to depressives.

"Keep talking," I said.

Carey said he hated being a developer and also didn't think he was very good at it; but he couldn't stop. "I have debts. Loans to repay. It's a lot. Don't ask how much. I don't really want to talk about it."

"Then don't," I said.

"Maybe this is the moment when I tell you that you should break up with me now if you want to—"

"I'm not breaking up with you."

"I'm opening the door for you. I'll understand."

"You're being dramatic is what you're doing."

"Run away—"

"Stop," I said and took his hand. "We'll get through it," I said.

He smiled at me: *we*.

When we were intimate that night, we were silent. Whereas before we each might coo with pleasure, and our volume might increase as our sex gained momentum, now we'd moved beyond any such signaling—we didn't need it—which made our lovemaking more intense, and which also made me feel more at risk. More was at stake; there was more to lose.

We lapsed into a narcotic drift: instead of replacing the fence at the bottom of the property or weeding the herb garden or finding new furniture for the terrace, we went on drives, one of us behind the wheel, the other saying go. There was the gaggle of orthodox school girls all covered up in their uniforms jogging around the reservoir. There were the two leathery muscle men riding in a convertible with the top down, the men too big for the tuna can of a car. There was a bakery truck. An

SUV with four bikes lashed upside down on its roof. We would follow someone awhile, then carom off to follow someone else. If this was the stranger game, it was our own version of it because we weren't talking about the people we chased; we weren't speculating about them or trying to achieve any empathic connection; we weren't saying much of anything. Like the first time we played the game together, we always ended up in a melancholy state, yet as soon as we got home, we'd end up in bed.

During the workweek, Carey would drop me off at the studio, where I had trouble focusing. I was supposed to be working through some concept drawings for a high-profile competition—some open land along the river was being transformed into parkland complete with recreation centers, and every firm who did what we did would be submitting a proposal—but I was making little headway, and I overheard my partners talking about how most tactfully to ask me to step aside from the project. At the end of the day, Carey picked me up, and while we had errands to run on the way home, instead we would follow a yellow bus packed with a middle school soccer team. We'd follow another bus: the field hockey players. We devised an iteration of the game wherein we picked up taxis and went wherever they went, fare to fare. We'd get home late. He'd start the shower. I'd get in with him. He'd pull me up against the slippery tile and we'd go at it with the water streaming down all around us. I couldn't get enough of him, of this. We were on a binge, and I started to think something had to give, although we weren't about to quit, were we, because the game only became more interesting to play.

One lunch break, we met up at the museum and were wandering the grounds, ending up at the sculpture garden. At the top of the steps (where I'd spied on Carey), we noticed a man and woman who were transfixed by two women standing down below in front of the steel dancing man. One of the women was quite tall, the other by contrast very short. The short woman dropped to one knee (making her even tinier compared to the tall woman); we could hear her (though barely) make a marriage proposal. She withdrew a velvet ring box from her pocket and a diamond band from the box. The tall woman gasped, allowed the ring to be slid up her long finger, and accepted by pulling the shorter woman to her feet and then hoisting her up so they were eye to eye and could kiss. All of us at the top of the steps clapped, and the now-engaged women blew us kisses. As Carey and I walked away, the man and woman who'd been standing next to us were locked in an embrace so intense I was fairly certain one of them would propose marriage, too. A happy story, the end—except it wasn't the end.

Two weeks later, all the way across town (and after many other random follows), Carey and I were walking along a pier at sunset and spotted a semicircle of people mesmerized by what we assumed would be a juggler or break-dancer. When we got closer, however, we could see the group was watching the very public display of affection between two women, one tall, one short—the very same two women we'd seen in the sculpture garden. The shorter woman was on one knee proposing to the other, apparently proposing again. One more time the taller woman happily lifted the shorter woman up in the air for a jubilant kiss.

I whispered to Carey, "Do you think they're—?"

"Definitely," he whispered back, and he nodded at another couple, embracing now as well—players, we decided, inspired to perform their own impromptu romantic show.

There was applause, and as the onlookers as well as the two stagers dispersed, I noticed that the embracing man and woman hadn't moved—indeed, the man was now kneeling (on both knees as if in prayer), offering his hand in marriage (or so it appeared, though without a ring). We walked away without knowing whether the woman said yes.

"So you think the guy hired the two women to stage a proposal," I said, "in order to sway his girlfriend so she'd say yes to him?"

"That's exactly what I think," Carey said.

"But why not simply propose? Why bother with the stagers?"

"Maybe the guy thought the woman needed incentive. Maybe he wanted a story to tell."

"How do you think one even goes about hiring stagers?" I asked.

"I'm not sure," Carey said, "but I bet you it's easier than you think."

THEN IT WAS JUNE, A SATURDAY MORNING. THE JACA-randas had lost their flowers en masse, leaving a layer of fetid purple blossoms everywhere. Light rain had made the air both cooler and more acrid, and before another storm moved in, Carey said he wanted to go out.

"Maybe a hike," he said.

"A hike would be perfect," I said.

"Actually." He hesitated. "I was thinking of going alone."

This took me by surprise. "Oh. Okay. I can't come with you? I need the exercise."

"It might be muddy," he said.

"Only a little muddy," I said.

Carey hesitated again, but then he said, "Okay, sure. Sure, come with. But we need to go now."

When we stepped out of my house, we noticed my neighbors across the street standing in their driveway and talking to two police officers. I didn't know these neighbors well (nor did I really know anyone on the block; most everyone had moved in within the last two or three years, displacing older people who had owned their properties for decades and decided to cash in on the real estate boom), but I walked over to make sure they were okay just the same. Carey hung back at first, then joined me. One of the officers told us that the house had been broken in to while the owners were out for a few hours, and that while there were a few crooked framed prints and a lampshade knocked awry, nothing appeared to have been taken. It appeared my neighbors' home had been burgled for burglary's sake. Had we seen anything or anyone suspicious casing the house? We had not.

Carey glanced at his watch. "There's nothing we can do for them," he said, and we expressed our condolences and concern and left.

Although he regularly played tennis in the park, Carey said he never ventured up into the canyon beyond the courts. I led the way. I took the slower ascent that wound around to a footbridge fording a ravine. Twice again I noticed Carey check his watch. Were we in a hurry? Did he have plans for us for after the hike? We passed almost no one else at the crest, and the path was a little more slippery than I'd counted on, making for a tricky descent. When we were on the western flank of the canyon with still a ways to go, Carey said he wanted to see the abandoned house. It was around the bend. It would rain again sooner than later. I didn't think we had time for the detour, but he was determined.

"It should be this way, right?" he asked.

"Right," I said and steered us down the side trail.

The house came into view, a brighter white in the cloudy weather. I nearly lost my footing but caught Carey's arm before I fell.

"What's your preferred rumor about what happened here?" he asked, and I was about to remind him about the article about the widow when we heard shouting.

It wasn't clear at first if it was coming from the house. Noise could rebound around the canyon in odd ways, its origin not always clear. But then two men, both of them lanky and bearded with strapped cameras bobbing off their chests, ran out of the house and up the slope, pushed through the gate, and sprinted back up to the main trail and scurried down along the property wall until they were out of view.

"Damn it," Carey muttered.

The sight of these two men plus more shouting sent him into action: he headed for the gate; I grabbed his elbow.

"Wait," I said, withdrawing my phone from my pocket. "I can call someone."

"You told me you couldn't get reception up here," he said and pulled free.

Had I given him that detail? He was already on the

other side of the gate when I threw up my hands and headed down the path, too.

"Wait," I called to him again, useless.

Then I heard a familiar low menacing voice: "You told me you were through with all that."

And a woman: "I said, let go."

Was it possible we were hearing the same stagers, the same routine? If so, we could relax: any distress was false distress, a hoax. No one was in trouble.

The man: "I trusted you. You swore it."

"Carey?" I whispered.

He'd entered the house the way I did the first time. I followed him in and went down the corridor, darker on a gray day, but I couldn't spot him in front of me.

"Where are you, Carey?"

I assumed he would be standing at the balcony and observing the two players for whom the scene was being enacted. In a few moments, our hero would leap into action.

The woman: "Why are you doing this? You stay there, you stay right there."

However, Carey was not standing at the balcony overlooking the lower room, and it was hard to see much of anything. At the railing, I peered down: there was the fireplace on the left, and someone else—someone by himself?—over on the right with the vantage of the terrace below.

The man: "Where are you going? Come here."

The woman: "I said, stay there."

I was confused. I could only locate one silhouette: Where was the second player who didn't know what was going on and would be impressed by her companion's valiant intervention? Had that part been played by the two bearded men who had already run off—they'd run off to get help?

My eyes adjusted and I could see Carey standing at the top of the stairs down to the next level. He was staring at the solo player, too. When I made it to his side and started to whisper, he shushed me.

Then the woman stager howled.

The solo player bolted out to the terrace.

Carey headed down the stairs and would have kept going all the way out to the terrace as well had I not grabbed his arm again at the bottom step.

"They're only stagers," I whispered. "It's theater."

My eyes adjusted once again, and the expansive terrace beyond came into view: the two men—the stager, the bald guy in the tracksuit, and the solo player, a man with silver hair dressed all in black—looked like they were trying to wrestle each other to the ground. With both hands, the bald man gripped the player's shoulders.

The woman—also the same stager with a ponytail, minus the wig—was moving away from the two men, who were locked in a peculiar two-step, one-two, one-two, moving gradually toward the edge of the terrace. It was drizzling now, everyone getting wet.

The woman said, "Wait, where'd they go?"

"They're gone," the bald man said. "This guy, this mother—"

The silver-haired player mumbled something inaudible.

"Stop," the woman shouted. "That's not what—" She didn't finish the sentence.

All of this was happening so quickly; Carey made a move toward the terrace, and one more time I held him back, this time shouting his name. And when I spoke, the silver-haired player on the terrace turned in our direction and gazed into the house.

The bald man's back was to us—he didn't swivel around. I noticed he was wearing surgical gloves, as white as milk.

The woman screamed, "Watch it!"

Everything was mixed-up. I was trying to keep Carey from lunging into the fray, and the silver-haired man was trying to wriggle free from the grip of the bald man and searching the house for us, for help, and he and the bald man were rocking closer and closer to the edge of the terrace, where there was no wall, nothing to catch the silver-haired man when, with a minor height advantage, he was able to shrug free from the bald-haired man's grip—or? Or the bald man released his hold on the silver-haired man. He pressed both gloved hands flat against the silver-haired man's chest, and pushed, once, hard, fast. So long.

The silver-haired man swung his arms around twice in turn as if swimming the backstroke, and then he fell off the terrace into the ravine below.

The woman clutched her forehead with her hand: What had they done? The bald-haired man looked down the slope beyond the terrace and turned back. He was the first up the exterior stairs, the woman right behind him.

I took out my phone—no reception—and Carey ran out to the terrace, then right up the steps after the bald man and the woman. Was he going to chase after them, or was he going to try to scramble down the rocks to where the silver-haired man landed?

I went outside, too, taking careful steps when I made it to the edge of the terrace, and when I reached the spot where the silver-haired man fell, I knelt down and tried to find him on the cascade of rock and scrub, the drizzle turning to rain. I couldn't see him. I scanned the lower trail for Carey—no sign of him either. Looking back down the ravine, I thought I spotted something now, a puddle of black fabric, flapping slightly in the wind like a broken umbrella. A body, a writhing body.

I ran up the steps, not seeing anyone: no stagers, no Carey, no other hikers to help me or go get help (and I could only hope the first two men who'd run from the house had reached the ranger's station). I had to go all the way up the property, turning my ankle in the mud, through the broken gate, and out and around the property wall in order to get access to where the silver-haired man was lying in distress.

All the while I was yelling, "Carey!" and, "Help, help!"

I have no idea how much time it took me to reach a point down the trail parallel to where the man had landed in the ravine, but I could see him now, the man on his side like he was taking a nap. There was no way I could get to him—or I could, but it would take a lot of careful climbing across soaked stone, and it made more sense for me to try to find the park police to summon a rescue team. When I looked up at the house to trace how far he'd fallen, the house appeared, in the way the moon did if you stared at it long enough, to be crashing straight down the hill, too.

One quick decision I made was that it would be faster to go back up the trail rather than down to the parking area. If I went up past the house, there was a park exit, and beyond that a road where I stood a better chance of flagging someone down. But trying to run up the trail in the rain, I couldn't get my legs to move fast enough. I had to pray that Carey hadn't gone after the players— to do what, to try to pin them and defeat them all on his own?—and that he'd had the better thought to seek help, too.

I reached the top of the hill, and as I was moving toward the exit, I saw three police officers pouring out of a truck that came up the road, three cops sprinting toward me, their guns drawn, their guns trained on me—

I held my hands up high, but I also was trying to wave them down.

"Freeze. Stop right where you are," one of them shouted.

I kept my hands in the air and shouted, "There's a man down on the rocks who needs help."

"On the ground," a second officer yelled.

"There's a man," I said. "He fell—he was pushed from the house."

"On the ground," the officer shouted again. "Hands on your head."

"Now," the first officer said, and I did as I was told, my knees sinking into the mud, the rain coming down hard now, a cold spring rain, which in a land of drought was always so desperately desired.

ONCE THEY FRISKED ME AND UNDERSTOOD WHAT I was trying to tell them and radioed for support, they treated me well, with one officer escorting me down the trail because I explained that was where I thought Carey might be. Even wrapped in a blanket and sitting in the back of a squad car, I couldn't stop shivering. Carey and I had driven up to the park in his car. His car was nowhere in the lot.

At the precinct house, I was allowed to exchange my soaked hiking clothes for a hoodie and sweatpants several sizes too big for me. The sergeant at the front desk volunteered to make me some instant ramen to warm me up, but I asked for tea. Meanwhile I told two officers everything I could about what I had witnessed and how I'd seen these stagers once before. I asked them how they knew to come to the house: Had Carey run down the trail to where he could get reception and called them? As far as they knew, the call came in from hikers who maybe had heard my screaming. Were they two men, two tall bearded men? The officers didn't know. While we were talking, they received word that the silver-haired man had been successfully transported to a trauma center.

"He's alive?" I asked, and they said he was, albeit unresponsive.

All I wanted to do was go home and take a hot shower and get in bed. The police, however, kept asking me to run through my account of what happened.

"You're saying the bald guy *shoved* the victim off the terrace?"

"It looked that way," I said. "If Carey was here…"

He'd offer his own version. It occurred to me that he might be in another room in the very same station. Would they tell me if he was? I asked; they said he wasn't there.

After an hour, the two officers were replaced by a detective; his posture was entirely different. Detective Allagash wasn't rude, but I wouldn't call him friendly. His single long eyebrow ran parallel to his mustache, forming an equal sign across his face. It was only the two of us in the room, a room in which everything was bolted to the floor, the steel table, the steel chairs.

"Ms. Crane," he said. "Rebecca, is it?" He pointed at a wall-mounted video camera behind him. "We're being recorded. Are you okay with that?"

I nodded yes. I wasn't told that they were recording our last conversation, so why was that happening now?

"Actually, Rebecca, I need you to say it aloud."

"It's fine," I said.

He had me run through my story yet another time. I tried to be patient. Detective Allagash, too, kept returning to the question of whether the victim had been pushed. He stood up and asked me to show him how it went down. I stood next to him and hesitated.

"Go ahead," he said.

I pressed my palms against the lapels of his ill-fitting herringbone jacket and said, "Like this." I pushed gently, but the detective didn't move, and I was the one who took a step back.

When we sat down again, Detective Allagash asked, "You were alone when you witnessed all of this?"

"No," I said. Wasn't he listening? "I was with my boyfriend." This was the first time I'd called Carey my boyfriend.

"And where is he now?" Detective Allagash asked.

"I think I told you, I don't know."

"You don't know."

"No."

"After something so traumatic—"

"He'll turn up," I said.

"Turn up?"

Where was he going with these questions? And then I pictured the bald man, his glowing surgical gloves flat against the victim's chest—surgical gloves that one wore for surgery obviously or… Or to leave no fingerprints, no trace. This was the moment when everything began to crash in on me, all at once.

"Turn up," Detective Allagash said, "like a lost cat—"

"Should I have a lawyer here with me?" I asked.

The detective leaned back in his chair. He stroked his mustache with his thumb and forefinger.

"Do you want a lawyer?" he asked.

"Do I *need* a lawyer?"

The detective started to say something, but I didn't let him speak.

"Can I call anyone?" I asked.

I still had my phone, although I'd been asked to turn it off and hadn't checked it since changing into the borrowed clothes.

"Would it be okay if I called another detective?" I asked. "Lisa Martinez, she's at a different precinct."

"Detective Martinez," Detective Allagash said. "You want to call *her*?"

He thought about it. Was he trying to suppress a smile?

"That's fine. Take what time you need," he said, and shut the door behind him.

When I turned on my phone to make the call, I noticed there were three messages from an unidentified number. I assumed they had to be from Carey (finally) and that for whatever reason he was using a phone he didn't normally call from. I didn't bother to listen to the voice mail and tapped the call-back button. It was not Carey who answered.

"There you are."

I couldn't speak.

"Hi, Rebecca."

I started shivering again.

"I'm sorry. I am so sorry—"

"Where are you?" I asked.

"Well, when I called earlier, I was visiting *Madame B*, but now I'm at the house—your house."

I couldn't hold it together. Too many thoughts. I started weeping.

"Ezra," I said.

"Hi," Ezra said, a small apologetic voice. "But wait. Rebecca. Where are *you*?"

3

INSTEAD OF SITTING ACROSS THE TABLE FROM ME, Detective Martinez carried a folding chair into the interrogation room and positioned it close enough for me to almost whisper what happened.

"I know you might still be in shock," she said, "so I'm sorry to make you keep talking, but there are some things here I'm not understanding. Why would Carey drive off and not come back?"

"Detective Allagash seems to think I made him up."

"Also we don't know yet who called 911."

"It might have been the two men who ran out of the house."

"And you think they were players?"

I had said that was what I thought, but now I wasn't sure. "But then who was the victim? Was he a player, too?"

"According to Allagash, the man didn't have ID on him. We'll check databases. We can try face recognition. As for the 911 caller, we have a cell we can track."

Normally the nimble reach of surveillance systems might bother me, but hearing this now made me feel like I had an ally in Detective Martinez.

"I told you Carey is my boyfriend," I said.

"You did."

"He's also the guy who was following me and ended up in my house that night. The one I mentioned when I ran into you by the dog park. Do you remember?"

Detective Martinez didn't blink. "I assumed as much when you told me."

"Oh," I said.

"Well, look, there probably is a good explanation about where he is. Maybe when he ran after the bald man and the woman, he slipped and fell—"

"He fell?"

"And he's fine," the detective said. "He's fine, but he's at urgent care—"

"Then he would have called," I said.

"Maybe he dropped his phone along the way."

This seemed plausible. "He'll get in touch."

"I bet he will."

"At which point, I'll let you know," I said.

"Please."

"Does Allagash think— Am I...?"

I didn't finish my question, but the detective knew what I was asking. "You're the only witness we have. You've been nothing but helpful."

"Do I need to find a lawyer?" I asked.

"You're not under that kind of scrutiny. How about I let you know if I think you should? Keep in mind though, I'm only your friend here. This is Allagash's investigation."

She was letting me know the extent to which she could get involved; she wouldn't interfere with her colleague's case; whatever leads he had were his to pursue.

"His approach can be rabbity," she said, "so be prepared for that."

"Rabbity?"

She didn't elaborate and stood up and straightened her gun belt.

"There's something else," I said. "Unrelated. Ezra. He called. He's back."

The detective sat back down, closed her eyes and shook her head.

"I know," I said.

She groaned.

"I know, I know, I know."

"Don't get pulled back in, Rebecca. Don't let him charm you. As if you don't have enough to worry about."

I was confused: Enough to worry about?

"I thought you were telling me not to worry—"

"I meant with what you've been through."

Detective Allagash opened the door but didn't step into the room.

"Detective," Detective Martinez said. "Anything new?"

There was not. I braced myself for a new line of questions, but instead a noticeably kinder Detective Allagash thanked me for my assistance so far and let me know where I could meet the officer who would give me a ride home.

"We'll be in touch shortly," he said. "We know how to find you."

ENTERING MY HOUSE I COULD SEE STRAIGHT ACROSS
the main room and kitchen to the back terrace, where
he was sitting in a chair facing the city at dusk, and my
first thought, even only studying the back of his head
and shoulders, was that Ezra occupied less space in the
world than the last time I saw him. He might have heard
me come in and turned slightly so I could measure him
in profile, but he didn't look back into the house. He'd
cut his hair short, although his chin was still dusted with
scruff. He looked gaunt. He was wearing a denim jacket,
the collar turned up on one side. My instinct was to step
outside and straighten it for him, or turn the collar up
on the other side, too.

I didn't want him to see me in the ill-fitting police
hoodie and sweats, so I skipped into my bedroom and
changed into jeans and a sweater. I washed my face
and tied my hair back. I rarely wore much makeup but

rubbed on a little lip gloss. By the time I stepped into the kitchen, he must have sensed my presence, because although he was still outside, he was standing and facing the house, his hands in his pockets.

I expected to cry the way I had when we'd spoken on the phone but didn't. He stepped inside; we hugged briefly. I wanted the embrace to mean less than it did.

"You went to the museum?" I asked, meaning he went to visit *Madame B*, but it sounded as if I were casually asking if that was where he'd been for nine months.

Ezra cleared his throat. He was the one who was teary. He nodded.

I put on a kettle. I couldn't look at him and busied myself finding mugs in the cupboard, selecting loose black tea, tamping it into the infuser.

"You were at the police station?" he asked. "Is everything okay?"

Was everything okay? Was everything *okay*? What was I doing? Oh, hi there, nice to see you, how have you been—I don't have any lemons, but would you like some honey in your tea?

"Rebecca?"

As the kettle was heating up, it sounded like a sudden gale knocking around skiffs moored in a cove.

"I was hiking and witnessed an accident" was all I said. "I was trying to help."

"An accident?"

I was leaning against a counter, not looking at him.

"How could you do that to me," I said.

Ezra had to have been expecting my anger. He let it come at him.

"All this time, nothing. Nothing from you. How unbelievably cruel," I said. And then I surprised myself: "I will never forgive you."

The kettle whistled and I let it go. Ezra stepped over to the stove and turned off the flame.

"And then you actually went to the museum," I said. "Thinking what, thinking I'd show up and take you home with me?"

Ezra shook his head no, no, he didn't think that.

"Your things are in storage, by the way," I said.

"Thank you," he said.

"And leaving your apartment like that for me to clean up, your car? Which I sold to pay for the storage."

"Rebecca—"

"What? What, Ezra, what?"

He had to clear his throat again. "I'm sorry," he said.

For some reason I nodded as if I were accepting his apology and continued making tea. The truth was I had nothing to say. I couldn't remember the last time I'd been this exhausted.

"Should I talk about it? Where I went," he said.

"You don't need to," I said. "I don't care."

"I can understand that."

"You should probably leave."

"I started playing the stranger game," he said.

"Yes, I figured that much out."

"Oh. You did?"

"You should go now. I'm expecting someone. He should be here soon."

As I announced this, it did seem entirely conceivable Carey would at any moment appear, limping, phoneless. I was getting more worried about him.

"I started playing one morning," Ezra said, "and I—"

"Ezra, I said I didn't care."

He nodded. "Right."

Boy, was I sending competing signals. I had asked him to leave and yet waited for the tea to steep and then poured him a mug. I headed for the sofa. As he sat down and set down his tea and placed his hands on his legs, he seemed thin again to me, his forearms all veins. I noticed his fingers were nicked, his hands calloused. He was darker the way he used to get in the summer, but not in a healthy way: more like the sun was aging him. This diminishment, this fragility—wasn't it my responsibility to protect him? And if ever I became infirm, wasn't he in turn supposed to look after me? I had become used to being on my own, but I couldn't claim that I'd worked out what it would be like to grow old alone. I needed not to think about this right now.

"You can tell me," I said, "but then I want you to leave."

So he did, in detail, and it took a while. As I listened to him, never commenting or asking questions, I had to push against my weaker desire to move across the couch to be next to him, to rest my head on his shoulder. After all, I had witnessed a man being pushed into a ravine; I could have used some comforting.

The last thing he told me was this: "I knew it would hurt you not knowing where I was. Of course I knew that. I thought it might help."

"Help? That's insane. Help how?"

"You used the word *cruel*. You're right. It was about the cruelest thing I could do," Ezra said. "If you hated me, you'd move on. Finally."

"It worked," I said.

Ezra grimaced a bit.

"I've been dating someone seriously. He's the one who should be here soon. He more or less lives here now," I said. "We're very happy."

Ezra knew me well enough to know I was withholding information.

"That's great," he said.

And I knew him well enough to know he was lying, too. After he left, I sat in the dark. I was hungry but didn't make anything to eat. I curled up and pulled an afghan over my legs, and that was how I slept, picturing Ezra on foot, in cars, farther and farther away—then retracing his steps, coming back to the city, back to me. This was the part of his story he left out, why he returned.

To describe the low point in his life he'd arrived at

before he started following strangers, A. Craig had written a line that had stayed with me: *How lonely and alone
I was*. Yes, this was that.

SOMETIMES WHEN I HAD INSOMNIA, I TRIED TO COAX myself to sleep by picturing in chronological order every bed I'd ever slept in, starting with the earliest I could remember, the wrought iron cot that I outgrew when my family moved when I was five, this first bed covered with a great-aunt's quilt and a blended family of teddy bears. Then in the house where I lived until heading off to college, I slept in a converted attic bedroom, the bed pushed into a corner beneath a sloped ceiling and angled in such a way that I wouldn't hit my head on a beam. There were the late-for-class/unmade-bed years in college, the first sex beds, the first boyfriend bed banked by skiing posters. The queen-size futon on a low frame that took up all of the space in my first apartment during graduate school, and a few other boyfriend beds, one belonging to an artist who made black paintings, these canvases the antithesis of snowy skiing posters; this was

the only time in my life when I consistently had night-
mares. There was Ezra's mattress on the hardwood floor
at his place, surrounded by used books and library dis-
cards; he had a better night if he took a hot shower before we went to sleep, and I would wait for him, paging
through outdated atlases. At some point, James the Cat
started nesting at the foot of my blankets, beneath the
blankets in winter. When I moved across the country,
James preferred sunlit rooms, and after a mild earthquake
started spending the nights under the modern plywood
bed I'd bought with an early paycheck, the same bed I
had now in the house on the hill, the bed Ezra joined
me in, the bed he left. There was the headboardless bed
in his apartment where I'd spent the night after the first
disastrous encounter with Carey…

Counting beds failed: I was wide-awake. I checked my
phone for messages. Carey hadn't yet emerged.

I tried to recall all of the hotel beds I'd spent a night
in, with or without Ezra, but mostly with Ezra in bed-
and-breakfasts and old city inns and oceanside motels
and a few grand hotels. It was three in the morning; I
wasn't really trying to fall asleep, was I? This felt more
like I was trying to summon renewed warmth for him
prefatory to forgiveness, but I needed to hold on to my
anger. I considered deleting his new number from my
phone. I also thought about calling him to find out where
he was staying. Instead of setting the phone back on my

night table, I got up and stashed it in a sock drawer, the best defense against temptation.

I did drift off and woke up with a hangover of anxiety and pensiveness. I had ended up in the center of the bed rather than staying on the side I preferred when sleeping with Carey. I smelled his pillows—nothing, no scent at all. I checked the closet: a few shirts on hangers, trousers, some recently folded laundry. This was the only trace of him. If everything were fine, he would have at least called me, and I pictured him unconscious in a hospital bed with a broken leg, no identification on him, no one knowing who to contact.

I made a quick list of nearby hospitals and then began calling. I realized I would need to claim a familiar or uxorial connection to get any information, and so I claimed the latter, deciding that if pressed I would say we were fairly newlywed and I had not taken his name. However, I wouldn't need to worry about presenting credentials because I reached five emergency rooms and no one fitting Carey's description had been admitted in the last twenty-four hours.

I stood under the shower a long while, almost lulled back to sleep, and when eventually I stepped out of my bedroom into the main room, I noticed a dark sedan parked in front. Detective Martinez had never come to my house before.

When she rolled down the window, I asked how long she'd been sitting there, and she said, "A few minutes."

"Would you like to come inside? I'll make coffee."

I noticed the detective was already holding a white cup in her lap. She raised a second at me.

"Do you have a moment?" she asked when she unlocked the door. "I won't stay long."

The latte wasn't too warm, which led to me to believe she'd been parked out front awhile.

"You could have rung the bell," I said.

"I didn't want to disturb you. We know the identity of the victim. His name is Carlos Garcia. A professor, retired. Does that name mean anything to you?"

"To me? No. Should it?"

"Not necessarily," Detective Martinez said.

"How is he?" I asked. "Is he conscious?"

"No, he's still critical."

"And do we know why anyone would want to harm him?"

"We do not, not yet."

"What about the 911 caller?"

"We have a name but haven't located him yet."

"Definitively not Carey," I said.

"That's correct."

"I called around to some hospitals to see if he'd been admitted," I said. "I mean, if he did fall or—or I don't know—"

The detective nodded. "I'm on it."

"Occam's razor," I said, wanting to appear sanguine.

The detective didn't respond.

"I mean as far as what happened to Carey. The simplest explanation—"

"Allagash thinks it's possible you pushed the victim," she interrupted.

"What?"

"It's one line he's following—"

"You're joking, right?"

"And according to Allagash, Carey is in hiding because he's afraid he'll get dragged into the investigation, and he doesn't understand why you did this, and so forth."

I was dumbfounded.

"I know," Detective Martinez said. "It makes no sense. That's why I'm telling you, which I shouldn't be doing."

"What possible motive would I have?"

"That's what I asked. Allagash wasn't more forthcoming."

The detective blinked.

"This is fucked up," I said.

"I agree, but Allagash is pursuing this, and maybe the best thing you can do for yourself is to find Carey."

"To corroborate my story."

"I'm looking for him, too," Detective Martinez said. "But you know him, his habits. You know where he hangs out, where he might lay low."

Did I?

"To be honest, I don't know what angle Allagash is working here," the detective said. "So can you do me a favor? Can you let me know if he talks to you?"

"I should probably have a lawyer with me if he does—"

"No," Detective Martinez said.

"No?"

"Not yet. I want you to tell me what questions he asks you. If you have an attorney, I don't expect he'd be as casual."

"But—"

"Can you do that for me, Rebecca? Please?"

Why was she asking this of me? Why couldn't she confer with him directly?

"I will let you know what he asks," I said.

"Thank you," Detective Martinez said. Not for the first time she added, "Please be careful," and not for the first time, I knew I would not heed her warning.

WHEN I WENT INTO THE STUDIO EARLY THE NEXT MORN-ing, my partner Rick was the only person there. He'd been designated by our other partners to ask me if I would take a leave. Given that cash flow was touch-and-go, it would need to be unpaid. I wasn't being asked if I would do this so much as told. It wasn't only that I wasn't bringing in clients and not completing the tasks I took on, but also that when I was in the office, I wasn't present.

"What do you mean I'm not present?" I asked, although I knew what he meant.

"You've been playing that game, haven't you?" Rick asked.

I hesitated a beat too long. "What game?"

"Oh, come on. I'm right, aren't I? You said you thought Ezra was playing, and you're all caught up in it, too."

I didn't want to lie to him but didn't confirm his suspicion.

"Sorry if I'm wrong," Rick said, "but it does seem like something has taken hold of you."

Then he handed me a card, the name of a therapist who specialized in treating people who had become obsessed with the stranger game.

"This is a specialty now?" I asked, and laughed.

Rick saw no humor in this. I pocketed the card and thanked him for putting up with me, promised I'd be back healthy and cured, and left without taking anything from my office. I had some savings, I could last awhile, but not forever, although I was too preoccupied to panic right then.

I walked over to Carey's office building, heading past the fountain in front and past the guard's desk, straight to the elevator bank like I knew where I was going.

The guard caught up with me. "Ma'am, you need to sign in."

According to the directory by the elevator, there were three media companies sharing the building along with accountancy and production companies, but no real estate firm as far as I could tell.

"Ma'am."

"I thought there was a developer with offices here, a real estate developer," I said.

"Come back this way, please," the guard said, ushering me to the reception desk, where I put the same question to someone wearing a headset.

"Not that I know of," the receptionist said.

"Has there ever been any kind of real estate office here?"

"Not that I'm aware."

"How about someone named Carey Taylor?" I said. "I should've asked that to begin with."

"We don't keep track of every employee," the receptionist said, "only the companies. The people come and go, but let me try something…"

She tapped at her keyboard, but nothing came up, and I didn't have a photo of Carey on my phone I could show her. I had no photos of him whatsoever.

"I did once follow him into this building," I said, right away regretting the comment: the receptionist now regarded me with some alarm.

I sat outside by the fountain and watched the water plume and recede. The guard kept walking over to the side of the revolving door to see if I was still there. Don't worry, I'm not a crazy woman, I wanted to tell him, except maybe I was.

I realized it was easier to believe Carey had been hurt and/or incapacitated because if that wasn't the case, then why hadn't he tried to reach me? In my mind, I replayed our interactions of the last few days; had I said something that had bothered him? Should I read something into the fact he initially wanted to go on the hike alone?

I had no idea where Carey lived, although I didn't think it was far from me because occasionally when he'd go retrieve something from his apartment, he wasn't gone long. How little I knew about him.

I headed over to the museum and peered down into the sculpture garden from above. There was the steel cube dancing man, the giant red tricorn hat.

I drove to the grocery where I'd once followed him.

Back home, I sat on his side of the bed and reread the texts he'd sent me, usually logistical. He would be at my place when. I needed what from the store. I had no saved voice mail from him—he never left me messages. The detective wanted me to find him to be my exculpatory witness; I wanted to find him to know our months-long affair was authentic, because now I was having my doubts. How insidiously trust leaked into the air, trust the thinnest of all gases.

Did I really think I'd find him again practicing his serve on the tennis court? It meant returning to the park, which made me unsteady. None of the courts were in use. I walked around the restrooms between the upper and lower courts. I stepped into the empty men's room. The doors had been removed from the stalls. Someone had scrawled graffiti: "Careful, snakes." As in: watch out, humans, be on the lookout for snakes? Or as a warning to the snakes themselves: beware, we're on to you.

I had no reason to believe Carey had even remained in the city, but I also couldn't understand why he would flee. He had to be nearby, he had to be. I thought I could find him, and the only method to do so that made sense to me was to wander around without a plan, although I knew that wandering around without any set destination was harder to do than it might seem. I needed some kind of vague scheme or I would only end up driving in circles through known parts of town.

The first lake I drove to sat in the hills a few miles west of the park. It was the one of three I knew about near me without having to consult a map, the farthest from where I lived. I drove around it twice, which was to say I drove around the street and looked at the garages of houses bordering the lake. There was a minor lookout though, a turnout where I could scan the water without getting out of my car. The lake was pale and unanimated, without any currents or ripples. Carey had said he wanted a house on a lake, and I knew he probably meant a lake in the mountains, but that didn't stop me from wondering if he was holed up in one nearby. I looked for real estate signs with the thought one might be on the market, it would be his listing, he'd have the keys, he'd hide there.

The lake nearest to my house was the reservoir, currently drained and weedy. There were signs explaining how it was being rehabilitated, the water supply secured underground in new massive tanks because that was the age we lived in; exposed drinking water was threatened drinking water. Above the buried tanks would be a shallow decorative pond behind a tall wire fence, not that it would matter if anyone got to it. I knew all of the houses around the reservoir well since this was where I ran, but I looked for Carey here.

Another lake, not far, was the only one where you ever saw paddle boats or children with toy boats. The park was empty now, too hot at midday, no one out.

I ventured farther out to the lakes at the edge of the city but still within the county limits. Another reservoir, another pale body with concrete banks. South in the county, there was a series of square pools where a marina had been planned and never finished. I crisscrossed the city three times in one day. Did I really think I would find Carey this way? No, but as long as I kept moving forward, I was able to quiet my mind.

I found several more lakes to visit the next morning, each smaller than the previous, odd blue parabolas interrupting the otherwise strict grid. I knew a heat wave flattening the city had to be why I was seeing very few people around, but I did check my phone to make sure I wasn't the only person who hadn't heard the news of a disaster, radiation everywhere, a toxic cloud. And in that scenario, did I really think the one other soul who would be out and about would be Carey? Would he pedal by on a bike? Would he be casting a rod into one of these fishless bodies of water?

All told I drove around looking for him for two and a half days. I say there weren't other people around, but I'm exaggerating, of course there were, and at one point, I noticed a small white hatchback in my rearview mir-

ror that I was fairly certain I'd caught a glimpse of the
day before, as well. I had to assume that once again I had
become the subject in someone else's game.

I had driven north and west along the spine of hills
through a gulch of newer homes and car dealerships to
a park where fast-growing eucalyptus dropped pods into
a pond to the point the pond looked littered with rep-
tile carcasses. I didn't get out of my car and instead tore
around a curved road and exited the park by a different
road than the one I'd entered. I didn't go too far into
the neighborhood before pulling over and waiting. And
there it was, the white car, peeking tentatively beyond
the park gate, also pulling over, its driver (whom I was
too far away to see in my mirror) holding back, probably scanning the road for me. I revealed my position by
driving forward fast and veering right at the first possible street. Again I pulled over and waited, and I saw the
white car come up the road past the turn I made. He'd
lost me. I swung into a fast U-turn, made the right, and
now I was the one following the white car, which after
five or six blocks pulled over again, the driver likely spotting me behind him.

I drove in slowly, not exactly wanting to scare him off,
and also unsure if I was up for a confrontation. Maybe
this was a dangerous idea. The closer I came, however,
the more I began to recognize the back of the driver's
head, hair once long, now short.

I slammed the door when I got out of my car and

marched over to Ezra, who got out from behind the
wheel of what I guessed was a rental.

"What are you doing?" I yelled. "You're following
me now?"

Ezra mumbled something I didn't understand.

"I saw you yesterday," I said. "You're pretty lousy at
this."

I had to wonder now what it must have looked like to
him, my zigzagging the city lake to lake.

"You're, what, concerned about me? Is that it?" I asked.

"I am," Ezra said, "yes."

"Don't be," I said.

"You've been driving—it seems like nowhere—all
day," he said.

"You said you played the game and disappeared as a
way to hurt me," I said.

"It wasn't the only reason—"

"A way to make me see once and for all what a
wretched soul you were so I'd move on. Except I don't
think that's what you were really up to."

I waited for him to correct me, but he didn't say anything.

"Maybe you sold yourself on the idea you were helping me, and this made you feel better about your selfish-
ness, but I had very little to do with it. You were only
concerned about your own destiny, not mine, not ours,
yours alone."

In the distance, a siren rose and fell.

"Say something," I said.

"I don't know what to say," he said. "Yes. You're right. Yes."

"You can't follow me, Ezra."

"I don't know what you're doing, and I'm worried," he said. "Something is going on. You're in over your head."

"Oh, fuck off. Fuck you for disappearing, and fuck you for coming back. If I see you stalking me again," I said, "I will get a restraining order."

When I drove away, Ezra was still leaning against his car. High overhead a dark chevron of long-tailed birds coasted north, and I wondered if he was thinking he should follow them back to where he'd found sanctuary.

WHEN WE WERE SITTING ON MY COUCH AND EZRA told me about the months he was gone, he said it was indeed from a fellow manager at the bookstore that he first heard about Craig's essay, although his colleague had described it disparagingly: Craig had walked away from the wreck that was his life and gone into hiding, and in the end, maybe he himself achieved clarity, but was the world a better place with strangers randomly chasing each other? Ezra said that no, it was not; privately he was intrigued. He couldn't remember how long he'd been running in circles, around and around past the same markers. And then he'd cooked me his mushroom risotto, and we'd looked at the art book, and had sex—*had* was the word Ezra used, and *had* was the right verb: to *make* love was to create something; to *have* sex was to answer a fleeting appetite, nothing more than consumption.

But it had been consequential, and Ezra admitted he

was miserable the next day. Would he ever come into his own? Could he make a life apart from me? He wanted to be remeeting me on a midsummer rooftop, our twenties ahead of us. He wanted never to have met me at all. He wanted to blame me for his unfulfilled self; blaming me, he decided, was childish.

One morning over breakfast, he said, he reread the printout of the essay. He packed his shoulder bag with his journal, pens, a spare T-shirt, a pair of boxer briefs, socks, and a few toiletries. He left behind his phone (no technology), as well as his car. He wore his best walking shoes and sunglasses and a baseball cap. He checked himself in the mirror before he left, squeezing the brim of the cap: Incognito Man.

The first person he spotted was a woman walking a big dog, the dog tugging the woman, who was having trouble keeping up. Ezra stayed on the opposite side of the street, a half block behind. The woman looked frail to him, and he speculated she'd recently survived difficult but successful surgery, survived in large part because she enjoyed the affections of this dog. But now that she was well, she found the dog tested her strength and—and what?

He didn't answer his own question because he was distracted by a man pushing a stroller his way. Ezra assumed he shouldn't make eye contact, but he did, in part because the father was familiar, an actor maybe. Both father and infant had espresso beans for eyes. When the man glanced back over his shoulder, maybe wondering what Ezra was up to, Ezra stopped at a bus shelter and sat on the bench. The only logical thing to do now was get on the next bus, which he did, and which carried him to the ocean.

It was easy to follow an elderly couple at the board-walk, the two of them loping along, unable to lick their ice cream cones before the ice cream melted. He was moved by how much they seemed to be enjoying each other's company. They stopped for a long while and watched a young man and woman lying out on the beach, and were they thinking this was them decades ago?

Ezra boarded another bus, this one headed up the coast. He ended up in a seaside town with thrift shops and diners. There were kids skateboarding during the school day. He watched a man clipping stems in the alley behind a florist. He watched a woman look at pottery in an antiques store, flipping every vase to check the price tag.

Another bus, one more town to the north. He fol-lowed two teenage boys into a movie theater and sat two rows behind them. The movie was nothing more than a sequence of detonations, but when he noticed the boys were holding hands, he was happy. I understood what Ezra meant when he said they filled him with vague hope about things. It was dark out when he emerged. He considered sleeping on a park bench, exposed to the salt air, but it was too chilly for that, and instead he found a cheap motel.

The next morning, a man in a baggy suit left the diner where Ezra had breakfast and got on a bus, so Ezra did, too. He liked the idea of riding buses regardless of the destination. Like me, he had always been a rule follower, and playing the game the way Craig had set it up came easily to him. In another seaside town, he picked out a mailman at random, then followed a guy wearing a narrow black tie and handing out religious pamphlets, then a martial arts instructor sweeping out his studio. He had nothing in common with any of these men, but he did his best to forge a connection: the mailman needed to finish his rounds early so he could run errands for an elderly aunt; the pamphlet distributor wasn't comfortable being evangelical, but he had to trust he would be in time; the sensei was worried about making the rent this month, what with fewer kids taking his classes, but it was best to stay busy.

Ezra spoke with no one he followed, which he didn't have to tell me ran counter to his natural outgoingness. At night he slept in inexpensive rooms. He wanted to keep his head clear and didn't drink any alcohol. He ate well enough but would pretty soon run out of cash. Each day he journeyed farther north. Each day he observed acts of kindness: a woman letting an older man check out before her at a grocery store, another woman helping another older (and confused) man get his bearings. A man refilling hummingbird feeders in front of his house. A guy who while walking his miniature pinscher had to stop, kneel, and give the dog a good nuzzle because he simply loved him so much. Humans were innately good; this was the conclusion Ezra wanted to convey to me, although this sounded less like a revelation than the renewal of a long-held belief. On a good day, Ezra said, he could go for hours without thinking about himself, surrendering his ego to empathy. It became clear to me as he was describing these nonencounter encounters that he was much more successful in playing the stranger game than I had ever been.

After a week Ezra lost track of time. He was living as the sun rose and set. He did suffer anxiety about the bookstore manager and colleagues he'd left behind. About me to an extent, although he needed not to think about me, not yet, he said. He calculated he had two more weeks before he would run out of money and would need to curve homeward, but he had the sense he was on the brink of transformation and wanted to keep going, to give himself over completely to the unpredictable, to surprise.

It was exactly two weeks later that he ended up sitting at the counter in a restaurant one hundred fifty miles north of the city and one hundred miles inland. A woman asked if the stool next to him was free, even though all of the other stools at the bar were unoccupied. Ezra noticed that she was carrying a mug of coffee with her, and it became clear that she'd been sitting in a booth by the window and maybe had been watching him. She asked if he had been traveling awhile. Yes, she suspected he had. She said he looked like someone who had no particular place he needed to be, and also that he was relying on public transportation—

Ezra had to interrupt. How did she know all of this about him? The woman was old enough to be his mother and was wearing a gauzy scarf and gauzy blouse that didn't seem heavy enough clothing for autumn this far north. Her lipstick was too orange for her complexion. Maybe she had been playing the stranger game, too, and now was breaking the rules. But no, he was wrong. The woman had a proposition. She had been driving all day and was dangerously exhausted. Her destination was still hours north, and she hated driving at night, especially on roads she didn't know. She was headed for an artist's colony at the top of a mountain, and she was wondering if Ezra could drive her the rest of the way. She would pay him, and give him money for an overnight stay somewhere and for his next bus fare.

Why did she trust him, Ezra wanted to know. Forget whether he was a rapist, how did she know whether he was a good driver? The woman, whose name was Lois, tilted her head and stared at him a long moment and said she didn't necessarily trust him, but her greater concern was getting where she needed to go. Although he never admitted it to the artist, Lois, her faith in him was flat-

tering at a moment when he needed flattery. He liked
the idea that he appeared dependable and open.

Ezra described Lois's small truck, the back packed
with rolled canvases, plastic bins of art supplies, and old
strapped luggage. She was chatty. She said she should tell
Ezra about the new body of work she would start at the
colony, but she hated that term, *body of work*, so preten-
tious. Did Ezra ever read the artist's statements in gal-
leries? He didn't? Good, they're awful. And what about
him, was he a creative (another term she deplored, an
adjective bent into a noun). Ezra said that despite aspi-
rations earlier in life, he was not a creative with a body
of work to speak of, and the woman said she liked him.
Lois told him he was young, he would figure everything
out, and Ezra said, Not that young. To which Lois re-
plied, Young enough.

The conversation wound on like this, but once they
reached the mountain several hours later, Ezra had to
concentrate on the narrow curves through the darkest
woods. When they arrived, Lois told Ezra to wait in the
truck while she checked in with the staff person who
had stayed up late to get her settled. Then Ezra drove
Lois down a dirt road to a cabin, her studio for the next
month, and he wasn't sure what would happen now.
Clearly there were no motels nearby. How would he get
down the mountain if he had to leave Lois's truck up
here? After he helped her unload her gear, Lois told him
colony residents were not supposed to have overnight

guests, but she'd gotten permission for him to stay one
night. Someone would drive him down the mountain in
the morning. Ezra surveyed the chilly open space, which
only had one bed pushed up against a far wall, the bed
wrapped in plaid blankets. Lois uncoiled her scarf. What
was she expecting now? But Lois said he could take the
bed and she'd nest in the loft. Ezra hadn't noticed the
ladder in the corner, the overhang of the loft. His as-
sumption embarrassed him, and he insisted on the loft.

The next morning Ezra said he found himself at a
long dining table with ten groggy artists and writers,
one composer, and one choreographer. Also two colony
managers who treated him as if he were one of the fellows. It was the beginning of the residency and no one
knew anyone else. Ezra explained he was merely Lois's
chauffeur, that he'd get out of everyone's way shortly,
but a poet told him he should at least take a hike on the
grounds. She'd been a resident before, and she said that
while the place was dressed in fog at the moment, in an
hour the most dramatic vistas would be revealed.

The colony sat on a thousand acres, half redwood, half
lush folding meadow, all of it sloping toward the ocean.
I could picture it; I could see how this landscape would
appeal to Ezra. When he returned to Lois's cabin to say
goodbye, she was setting up easels and arranging her
paints and brushes on tables, and she told Ezra the colony was hiring, and he was out of money and needed a
job, right? Ezra didn't remember telling her any of that

the night before. Then Lois said, You can't keep playing that silly game forever, and Ezra released a single *ha*. How did she know? Lois shrugged and said she was no psychic, just old. Not that old, Ezra said, and Lois said, Old enough.

It turned out that the on-site groundskeeper and occasional handyman had unexpectedly quit. What did Ezra know about clearing trails? Nothing. What did he know about fixing cabinets and replacing tractor tires? Again nothing, even less. Did he have a problem with rattlesnakes? Yes, actually. Did he enjoy being outside all day long? Maybe, as long as it wasn't too cold or rainy. Terrific, the colony manager said, you're hired. Ezra would receive a modest salary, a small cabin to himself, and meals.

So this was where the stranger game had led him. (It reminded me of the way A. Craig ended up at the desert inn.) His days, his weeks became about donning work gloves and mud boots and taking a chain saw to brush to keep the trails clear for the fellows to wander when they emerged from their studios. Other crew came and went, and he learned to do things like change the tire of a riding mower and replace a broken window pane. He loved this; he absolutely loved working with his hands, and the best part was when occasionally he got to help a sculptor collect branches and stones and other natural detritus for her assemblages. At night he hung out with the chef who came to make dinner, and sometimes he played board games with the fellows, although the one rule was that no matter how interested he might be, he could not ask them about their work; he only discovered about the cantos and epics and prints and videos they were making if they chose to talk about them, which sometimes they did.

I asked if being around all this art production made him long to be writing again; he said it did not, not really. Though he was beginning to see a role for himself in the world that had to do with supporting and celebrating artists, but not with making anything. He wasn't sure; his ideas were still fuzzy. And there was an artist who gave him a few life-drawing lessons. I asked what or who Ezra drew, and he said, trees—and from memory.

After a month, all of the fellows departed, including Lois, who insisted Ezra come visit her when he needed a vacation; she was a good cook; she'd invite her unpartnered friends; she'd set him up. After all of the hugs goodbye, Ezra thought about leaving, too, but as far as the colony manager was concerned, he had work to do to help prepare the studios for the next group of fellows who would arrive in a few days.

It was during this interstitial period that Ezra said he became involved with the assistant colony manager, a younger woman who was a painter, and who on her days off went to see a boyfriend who lived two hours away; they had an arrangement for now, for as long as they were living apart. Ezra was uncomfortable at first for a lot of reasons—a coworker, a woman who wasn't really available—but in many ways this worked. He was shy about telling me the details, but in some ways it was a relief knowing he'd found comfort somewhere; it didn't sound complicated.

Another month, another cohort of fellows arrived. The colder months meant more time indoors. There was a library in the main house where the meals were shared; Ezra read and reread classics. He continued to tend to the grounds and take hikes. The colony sat atop a mountain, but the mountain seemed like nothing against the endless ocean; the ocean reminded him of how small he was in the world, he said, and I got the sense Ezra was enjoying a kind of self-effacement, an erasure, a starting over.

Another month—but it wasn't all paradise. Ezra was lonely, deeply lonely some nights. (The assistant colony manager quit and went to live with her boyfriend, and an affable replacement came in instead, but not someone with whom Ezra would want to get involved sexually or romantically, which was for the best anyway.) And one night when he was up drinking whiskey with the choreographer-in-residence, Ezra opened up about me and what we'd been through and what happened when we were last together. You mean you left without telling her? the choreographer asked. That's horrible. Well, Ezra said, we had a complex history— Horrible, the choreographer insisted. I'm sure your plan worked, I'm sure she hates you now, nice work.

The next day the choreographer apologized for her
bluntness, but Ezra said it was good to be reminded that
he'd been terrible and he'd pay the price in time. Your
ex-girlfriend might be worried, she might think you're
dead, the choreographer said, and Ezra said he knew that
I knew he was alive; that much he was sure about. Then
she might wish you were dead, the choreographer said,
which she probably meant as a joke but which made Ezra
miss me in a way he could no longer deny. At this point,
he'd been gone seven months and worked the winter
at the colony and begun to see the wildflowers bloom.
For several years, Ezra and I would drive out of the city
when the poppies opened.

I wanted to know why, if he missed me so much, he
stayed at the colony another two months, and Ezra said
his goal was a year—could we be apart a year? Could
he go one year without seeing me, talking to me, joking with me, confiding in me, being less lonely around
me? Hugging me, holding me, making love to me. And
then he loathed himself for being so pathetic, so selfish, for wanting to reknot us to one another, and why
on earth would I want that, too? Of course I would not
want that, especially not now. I didn't know what to say
when he told me this, so I said nothing.

Finally he couldn't stand being away, and after nine
months he gave notice and rented a car and headed south,
arriving at the museum, calling me from the room with
my favorite painting, idiotically romantic, ridiculous yet

hopeful, calling me and leaving messages and then driving to my house, but not using his key to let himself in
because that breach of privacy of all things was a line he
could not cross.

I'd been so mean to him when I discovered him following me in his rental car, maybe because I didn't want
to explain my folly or appear helpless—certainly not like
I needed *his* help. Or maybe because it wasn't Ezra whom
I wanted to materialize and express care and concern; it
was Carey I wanted to see. I arrived home in a worn-
out state, which didn't make me as sharp as I should have
been when I pulled into my driveway at the same time
Detective Allagash with a crew of uniformed officers
approached my front door, a search warrant in hand,
his brow and mustache forming twin parabolas when
he frowned.

I STOOD IN THE DOORWAY TO MY BEDROOM AND watched two police officers pluck Carey's clothing from my closet, hangers and all, and drop it into plastic bags. A third officer walked around my house with a comb and tweezers. The detective wanted to speak with me out of earshot from the other cops, so we stepped onto the back terrace.

"This Carey Taylor," he said.

"You're going to tell me that's not his real name," I said.

"For starters."

"Well, you have his shirts now, so you can see he's tall. Sleeves for days."

"We've canvassed the neighborhood," Detective Allagash said. "No one seems to know him."

Picturing the police questioning my neighbors made heat rush to my cheeks. I had nothing to hide yet still suffered some measure of shame.

"I've never been very chatty with my neighbors," I said.

"None of the local restaurant people know about him either."

"Really? We ate out often enough," I said. "How did you describe us?"

Detective Allagash was staring at me skeptically.

"I didn't invent him," I said. "You've got his clothes now."

"Oh, we'll figure out who they belong to," the detective said.

He went inside, and I stayed on the terrace until his men were done, which didn't take long. They were quick and tidy and at most displaced the throw pillows on the couch.

Before he left, Detective Allagash said, "Please don't think about going anywhere without letting me know first. We'll be wanting to continue our conversation."

I called Detective Martinez right away.

"What did the warrant say?" she asked.

"The warrant," I said.

Detective Allagash had waved a folded white page, but he hadn't given it to me, and I hadn't read it. This was embarrassing to admit.

Detective Martinez scolded me: "Do you not watch police shows on television?"

"Is he trying to intimidate me?" I asked. "Trick me into saying something?"

"Shake a tree, fruit falls out," she said. "It's possible. By the way, I located several Carrie Taylors, all women, but only one male Carey Taylor, and he was seventy-two."

The reception wasn't great and I was having trouble hearing her.

"Where are you?" I asked.

"I'm an hour south, driving back. I interviewed the 911 caller."

"You talked to them, not Detective Allagash?" It was still his investigation, wasn't it?

"Right" was all Detective Martinez said. "There were two of them, tourists from out of town," she said.

"The two men we saw running away from the house," I said.

"They were fake playing the game. You know what I mean. One of them hired the stagers, the other had no clue what was going on."

Apparently the one who'd arranged and paid for the stagers was deeply embarrassed about being a player and didn't want to tell the police at first. They were in the middle of the prearranged follow at the abandoned house when Garcia appeared out of nowhere (although the tourist later realized that he had been following him and his friend for at least as long as they were hiking). Garcia started yelling something at them too rapidly for the two men to understand, and sensing they were in danger, they fled. And as they were heading down the trail, the men looked back and saw the old man fall from the terrace.

"The first one, the one who had arranged everything,"

Detective Martinez said, "called 911. But they got nervous, worried maybe they'd broken the law, so they ran."

"And we have no idea what Garcia was shouting," I said.

"Not really. It was only clear that he wanted the game to be over."

"I can't figure any of this out."

"That's not your job," Detective Martinez said.

"But—"

"I'm working on something. Call me again if Allagash comes back. And, Rebecca, please—"

"Be careful," I said.

"Yes."

Nightfall came late and was a relief in a way; at night I could focus better. Allagash didn't have a workable theory or he would have questioned me again or even arrested me. Martinez did not seem to be collaborating with him, but why? And why did the man named Garcia need to stop the tourist players and the bald stager, and why was the bald stager wearing surgical gloves, and had I even seen that correctly? I no longer trusted my own memory. Carey could verify my story, if only he existed as the man I thought I'd known—but who was he? My confusion about why he had vanished, my worry something had happened to him, was turning into something else—hurt that he had abandoned me, anger.

I was startled when my phone rang some hours later. I'd fallen asleep on the couch.

"I apologize for bothering you so late," Ezra said.

"It's fine," I said. "I'm sorry about how mean I was before. I'm still mad, but I'm also sorry I yelled."

"Oh," Ezra said.

"That's not why you're calling?"

"No, I'm calling because a detective came to see me—"

"Allagash," I said.

"That wasn't her name."

"Her? Martinez?"

"Yes," Ezra said. "I should have told you earlier."

I was fully up now and pacing.

"She wanted to know if I'd ever met someone named Carlos Garcia," Ezra said. "Who is Carlos Garcia? Actually never mind. I don't need to know. She wanted to know if he was someone in our world or someone maybe you'd met after I left."

Hold on: Someone I had met?

"What else did she want to know?" I asked.

"She asked me about your mental state."

"You mean whether I'm delusional?"

"Or depressed," Ezra said. "She wanted to know what you'd told me about the guy you were dating. And when I'd last seen you."

"And you told her about how I was driving around and caught you following me."

"No, I talked to this detective yesterday morning before I started following you, not today," Ezra said. "I don't know how she knew where I'm staying, but she found me."

I could see now how the conversation with the detective had made Ezra troubled enough to trail me, but what I couldn't understand was why Detective Martinez didn't tell me about talking to Ezra when I'd spoken with her earlier. Why was she involving him at all? Didn't she believe me? Was she investigating me, too?

"I didn't call you yesterday because I know you don't want me contacting you, but I was thinking about it and decided you should know," Ezra said.

I was nodding, although of course Ezra couldn't see me trying to say thank you.

"And that's all I'll say. She only talked to me for a few minutes. I'm sorry I bothered you. I promise I won't anymore," he said, and hung up.

I was more baffled than ever. I'd thought Detective Martinez was my ally, but maybe not. I no longer knew who to trust.

DAYS OF SILENCE FOLLOWED, SOME THE LONELIEST I'D
known. Days speaking to no one, never leaving the house,
working my way through whatever provisions were in
the pantry, soup, crackers, pasta and bottled sauce. Finally
one afternoon I had to go down to the grocery store, and
I lapsed instead into some shadow version of the game,
following strangers but never speculating about the man
taking phone photos of the racks of spice bottles, in no
way trying to connect with the woman who kept having to replace the bottom-shelf bags of grain her toddler
pulled onto the floor. Out on the street, I watched a kid
practicing soccer tricks at the bus stop, a woman clutching a bouquet of daisies behind her back.

I stopped wandering when I noticed a lost dog flyer
stapled to a telephone pole. A wire-haired terrier, big
eyes. I wondered what I looked like as I stood there on

the sidewalk crying. Perro perdido. I tore off the please-contact-if-found phone number.

At home I put away my groceries, but then I went on a walk because I was convinced that somehow I would be the one to find the terrier. Before the day was out, I would be the neighborhood hero. Hi, you don't know me, but I think I have Stuart here. No, it would be my pleasure to bring him back to you.

The streets around my house looped in on themselves, and something odd happened when walking roads usually driven. Why had I never stopped to look at that magisterial eucalyptus before, growing at a dangerously acute angle, raining pods on the several houses beneath its reach. Was that tarp-covered motorboat always parked in that driveway?

I didn't expect to find the dog, but I also didn't expect to observe this: about a mile from where I lived, a half block up from where I was walking, I noticed a sports car drift out of a concrete garage attached to a concrete modern house, turn up the street, and vroom off. Right as the car disappeared, a man and a woman emerged from a parked car and shuffled over to the concrete house. They did not ring the doorbell. Instead they went around the side of the garage, reached over a gate to unlatch it, glanced around, and then stepped into the backyard. The way they moved, fleet, almost on tiptoes, one shushing the other, reminded me of all of the followers I'd followed—but they weren't in pursuit of strangers; it looked like they were breaking in.

I waited for them to reemerge carrying a television or computer or other loot, but that didn't happen. I waited a little longer. I had my phone ready to call the police, although I'd had enough of the police and was not interested in playing the good samaritan. Then I heard splashing.

I approached the house now, too, peered through a gap between the gate and gatepost, and saw the pool in back. Two piles of clothes lay on the decking. Both the man and the woman were skinny-dipping.

I went back out to the street and noticed that in the time I'd been spying on the trespassers, a squad car had parked across the street. No siren, no flashing lights. Maybe neighbors had witnessed the break-in and called. The sole officer in the squad car wasn't getting out. He was watching a video on his phone. When I approached, he seemed reluctant about rolling down his window.

I explained what I'd seen, being sure to add, "I'm not entirely sure what's going on, but I know there have been burglaries recently in the neighborhood."

The officer said, "Thank you very much."

I didn't understand. "You don't want to check out what they're doing?"

"Thanks for your help, ma'am," he said. "Thank you very much."

"Are you off duty? Should I—?"

"Everything is fine, ma'am. Have a good day."

And with that the officer rolled up his window and stared at me until I turned around and began the uphill walk home.

I FOLLOWED A TOW TRUCK DRIVER AND WATCHED HIM haul off a car from a no-parking zone. The tow truck driver stopped at a taco stand for lunch, his truck now in a no-parking zone of its own with the towed car exposed for all the world to see.

I followed two girls on bikes who sat back with their hands off the handlebars so they could gesture to one another. They weren't wearing helmets, and I should have but did not break the rules to tell them this was stupidly unsafe. Maybe I envied their invincibility.

I followed dog walkers and nannies dragging along preschool children and gardeners, all of the noonday caretakers on their rounds.

I followed furniture delivery trucks and watched crews carefully fold up padded cloths postdelivery with the same care and reverence afforded flags.

There were other delivery trucks, flowers, pizza; there

were taxis. People on cell phones walking down the street, people carrying dry cleaning and cake boxes. I followed a fire truck returning to its station.

It was summer now and I was driving around with the windows up and the air conditioner on high, which muffled street sounds, which intensified my isolation. I kept checking my mirrors to pick up followers, but I never caught anyone, not that I cared. Go ahead, follow me, follow the woman who needs a haircut and has circles under her eyes, the insomniac talking to herself. I was never home; I kept moving. Motion made it possible for me to avoid the swelling resentment I felt with each passing day that Carey didn't surface.

When my phone rang and it wasn't him calling, I let it go to voice mail. Once it was Detective Allagash reminding me I should not leave town without informing him. I expected to see him at my door again, but he hadn't returned. Three times I didn't return Detective Martinez's call; she, too, didn't appear as I expected she might, coffee in hand. I knew I couldn't put them off forever.

I was spending my days driving in circles around the city, sometimes along familiar streets, often not, and this was how one afternoon I found myself in a neighborhood I didn't know well, coasting along a boulevard lined with fabric and furniture stores. Traffic was dense, but we were all moving, and I drove past a packed sidewalk café and noticed two men huddled at a small table—I think I gasped, although no one could hear me, least of all the two men.

One of them was the bald man in the tracksuit whom I'd last seen pushing Carlos Garcia off the terrace of the abandoned house. And sitting across from him was a tall man, rakish with wheaty hair mussed up by the breeze. He leaned in and said something it looked like he wanted no one else to hear. It was Carey.

It was the bald guy, it was definitely the bald guy, and it was Carey. Together.

I couldn't stop. There were no open parking spaces to slide into, and there were cars backed up behind me. I turned the corner and sped up the block, turned right and right again, and came fast down the narrow side street, which was treacherous with cars coming at me in the opposite direction. There was nowhere I could stop, and as I turned back on the boulevard and drove past the café a second time, I saw Carey stand up and wag a finger at the bald man. He was wagging his finger and then pointing it at him, the bald man standing, as well. I couldn't tell if they were making a scene, if anyone else at the café overheard them or wondered if there was a disturbance—

I honked. The driver in front of me on the boulevard gave me the finger. I couldn't see if Carey or the bald man looked in my direction—I had gone too far down the block now. I zoomed around a third time, but when I reached the sidewalk café again, determined to double-

park if I had to and jump out, both Carey and the bald guy
had vanished. Their table was being cleared for waiting patrons, and I wondered for a moment if I'd seen them at all.

But I knew I wasn't imagining them; I knew this was
them together, arguing; I knew, I knew, I knew it was
them.

I could not yet understand Carey's deceit, not with any
clarity. I had to drive a ways before finding a place to
pull over, and when I did, first I opened my car door and
threw up on the pavement. Then I took out my phone.

"Oh," Ezra said, surprised, "hi."

"I need to see you," I said.

4

"THIS IS ALL MY FAULT," EZRA SAID.

We were sitting on my couch. All of the windows were open, and the air both inside and out was warm and heavy and still.

"If I hadn't disappeared," he said, "would you have ever become a player?"

"I still could have been buying a sweater," I said, "and Carey still could have started following me. I still could have met him at the bistro."

Ezra knew everything now, likely in more detail than he wanted.

"What a fucking fucker," he said. "Whoever the fuck he is. What do we do now? We don't know Allagash's next move."

We was good to hear, I had to admit.

"By now he's probably destroyed Carey's clothing," I said, which probably was a felony, but I somehow didn't think Allagash exactly followed the law. "I don't know why, but I think he wants to eliminate any connection to Carey."

"And Martinez," Ezra said.

"What about her?"

"Why did she keep telling you not to get a lawyer?"

That I didn't know. It had become confusing to me, too. Maybe I had wrongly assumed the detective's interests were the same as my interests, but why would they be?

"Maybe we should get out of town for a while," Ezra said.

"Allagash told me not to go anywhere," I said.

"It sounds like he said not to go anywhere without telling him. You can still tell him. Or not."

"That man, the bald guy, he *pushed* someone into a ravine. Shouldn't he be accountable for that?"

"Of course," Ezra said. "But that's not our problem."

"You didn't see it happen," I said. "If you saw it happen, it would be your problem."

The winds from the west were picking up, sweeping up the hill and rustling the scrub so it sounded like a legion of small animals was suddenly charging the house.

"I'm glad you called me," Ezra said. "I'm glad you told me. My fear is that you want revenge, but…"

But what, he didn't say. That revenge would be misguided and dangerous? It would. However, I couldn't abide playing the victim: once a victim, always a victim. That would forever be how I thought of myself.

"I need to make sure you don't do something foolish," Ezra said, well-intentioned but a bit patronizing to my ear.

Now the wind was *in* the house and tipped over a standing lamp with a rice-paper shade. I got up to close the back door. When I returned to the couch, I sat closer to Ezra. I would have liked to have said he no longer had the ability to calm me down, but he did.

"That was a big sigh," he said.

"I really am sure I saw them together quarreling," I said, although even as I reasserted this, I was beginning to question my own hold on reality.

"I believe you."

Maybe he was right; maybe we should sneak off. We could walk down the hill to the boulevard and take the first bus, another bus, a random follow, another, see where we ended up.

"There's a lot about the stranger game we don't know," Ezra said. "The stagers, their network. How people hire them and then how it works."

"Martinez could tell us, I'm sure."

"I don't think we should talk to her," Ezra said, and I had to agree with him. "But I have an idea," he said. "Someone we can ask."

THE PSYCHOTHERAPIST WAS ABLE TO SEE US THE NEXT morning even though it was a Sunday. His carriage-house office was only a ten-minute drive. I didn't think at first that I'd saved the contact that my partner Rick had given me, but Ezra knew my habits and knew to check the wooden bowl atop my bureau where I tended to toss stray business cards and buttons. Ron was the therapist's name, and he sat so tall in his wing chair facing us on a long leather couch, it looked like he was holding court from a throne. Ezra and I had cooked up a story, which I had fed Ron when I called him: a close friend had become addicted to the game. In order to help, we wanted to understand it better, and then, since this was his specialty, maybe Ron could facilitate an intervention, et cetera.

But Ron said to help him help us help our friend, he wanted to know more about our own personal histories, together and apart. I gave him as brief a summary as possible.

When it was Ezra's turn, he said, "Actually, Ron, there is no friend. Or what I mean is, I'm the friend."

I glared at Ezra. I didn't see how we'd get the information we wanted if one of us claimed to know too much about the way the game was played.

Ron looked at me. "Rebecca, is this true?"

"It's true," I said, "but I got into the game as well, arguably in deeper than Ezra."

"She only became a player because of me," Ezra said.

"I'm my own person," I said, "fully capable of making a mess of my own life."

"As you might imagine," Ron said, "your stories are not unfamiliar to me. If I had a dime for every so-called friend who ended up where you're sitting now…"

This was the problem I had when I had sought out therapists in the past, the way everything I recounted about myself inevitably fell into an easily recognizable behavioral pattern. Yet what if I thought of myself as unique and took no comfort in being like other people, the opposite? Wouldn't it be more productive in getting me to open up to allow me my delusion?

"Ezra, what was your experience with the game?" Ron asked.

I had to listen again to Ezra go through his entire story about life at the colony.

"And you came back because you wanted to be with Rebecca," Ron said.

"I am so sorry," Ezra said to me.

I knew that. I didn't mean to be cruel, but I wanted to get the conversation back on track.

"Rebecca, what does hearing Ezra's apology mean to you?" Ron asked.

"Oh, I don't know," I said. "Neither one of us was really that far gone. It's not like we ever hired a stager. It's not like we're even sure how to do that."

Ron waited for me to say more.

"How does one do that anyway?" I asked. "Hire a stager."

Ron studied us, tilting his head ever so slightly to the left, then the right.

"Some couples like yourselves come to me to figure out how to live apart," he said, "but I want to ask if in fact the opposite might be the case for you? Do you think that's what you might be seeking this morning? A new commitment?"

"Oh, man," I said.

I hadn't been aware of my body language, my arms crossed, my legs crossed. Ezra's hands were palm down on the couch, pressing into the leather as if he were about to spring forward.

"When we were still together and I was alone in our house," I said, "I used to walk from room to room and run my fingertips over the furniture, over certain objects. A matte green vase from the year we were going to flea markets, or a hammered-tin Christmas star from a trip abroad, or even the lavender on the terrace that I'd watched Ezra pot and water and tend to. I'd touch these things, I think, to verify that they were real, and they were, and I would be so happy, so unbelievably what-did-I-do-to-deserve-to-be-this-happy happy. I loved our life together."

Ron smiled at Ezra: look how well this is going. Your turn.

But I continued, "And then Ezra would come home from the bookstore, and he'd be in another gray mood, and none of this seemed to matter."

"She could be happy when I wasn't home," Ezra said. "Not when I came home, not *because* I came home."

"That's not what I meant," I said.

"Have you sought couples counseling before?" Ron asked.

"Briefly," I said.

"I'm the problem," Ezra said blandly. "I am always the problem."

But he had disappeared for most of a year—wasn't that problematic?

"It takes two to make or unmake any relationship," Ron said.

"I don't mind being on my own now," I said. "I don't have to feel guilty about wanting what I want. I can simply want it."

My words were darts, I knew this. Ezra was now the one with his arms crossed.

"Let's try an exercise," Ron said.

"Actually, Ron, let's not," Ezra said, back with the program. "We really do have a friend, a player. Much worse off than us, which is why we came to see you."

"Much, much worse," I said.

"He's lost his job, his girlfriend," Ezra said.

"His house," I said.

"He's depressed, but he can't stop playing," Ezra said.

"He's someone you worry about becoming," Ron inserted.

Ezra waited a beat. "There but for the grace," he said.

"And he became a stager," I said. "Our friend."

Ron shook his head and said, "Honestly, I'm not as worried now about the stagers as I am the trespassers."

"The trespassers," I said, as if I knew what he was talking about. "I know, right?"

"Hopefully your friend isn't getting into that, too," Ron said.

And then I understood. I pictured the couple I'd seen sneaking into that backyard and skinny-dipping. And then there were all of the other break-ins in my neighborhood, yet nothing was ever reported stolen—the spying, the entry, that was the ultimate follow.

"It used to be seduction," I said, "that was the endgame. Now this."

"Who knows where it will all lead," Ron said.

"Now that I think about it, given some things he's told us, I realize that our friend has indeed been trespassing," Ezra said with such conviction that I almost asked him which friend.

Ron held Ezra's gaze a long moment. "I think we both know your *friend* needs to stop that immediately."

For the rest of the session, which was only introductory and therefore thankfully brief, Ron described his methodology. He likened any long-term couple to two sticks of chewing gum, which over time in the same mouth inevitably became one piece. In the months ahead, we would try to pull the gum apart to restore the two sticks so that moving forward they could exist in the same mouth with mutual love and respect. Or something like that. To be fair I was only half-listening, and I knew Ron meant well, and I probably shouldn't have said what I said after we told him we'd call soon to schedule a full session.

"And I guess the problem with chewing gum is that at a certain point it completely loses all taste."

Ron looked at me with round forgiving eyes: We have a long road ahead of us, don't we?

Ezra and I sat for a while in my car without saying anything. Per usual I had no clue what he was thinking. We had scheduled the time with Ron to see what we could learn about the stranger game, not to relitigate old cases against each other.

Finally Ezra said, "I didn't hate our life."

"Well," I started to say.

"How long do you want me to feel miserable?"

This took me aback. "Excuse me?"

"How long—"

"I heard you," I said. "You disappeared for nine months and left behind your car and your belongings, and I'm somehow not supposed to be devastated or angry or—"

"I mean how long do you want me to feel miserable for leaving after years when everything wasn't so perfect and lovely for me as it was for you? I mean how long should I feel miserable for not being able to keep up with you?"

I had no idea how to respond to this, so I didn't. We took turns sighing, and then silence again. We needed to return to the reason we'd sought out Ron.

"I told you about the people skinny-dipping," I said.

Ezra sat up, grateful for the subject change.

"You said they looked like players," he said.

"And I told you about the squad car parked across the street. The officer didn't care."

"Because he knew what was going on. Wow."

"He was guarding them," I said.

Everything was crashing together now. It made sense; it didn't make sense.

"The cop was paid off," Ezra said. "The cops are in on it."

"In on—?"

"The whole damn thing," Ezra said.

"No, I don't believe that. I don't think it's possible,"

I said, although I was starting to believe it was indeed
very possible.

"We need to find out."

"I don't know—"

"I'm telling you, think about it—"

"Okay, okay, let's see what we can learn," I said, pulled
out my phone, and tapped the number for my last missed
call, for the last three missed calls.

"Finally," Detective Martinez said.

THERE WERE NO CARS ON THE STREET BY MY HOUSE, so I was very startled when I saw Detective Martinez standing out back taking in the view. Where had she parked?

"Would you like to come inside?" I asked. "I can make some tea."

The detective eyed Ezra warily.

"You've met," I said.

"Let's stay out here," Detective Martinez said. "Allagash had his guys sweep the house, right?"

"Right. Why?"

Oh. It had never occurred to me they might have planted listening devices. Now I had to worry about everything Ezra and I had talked about having been overheard.

"Let's speak alone," the detective said.

"It's okay. He knows about everything," I said.

"I'd rather speak to you alone."

"It's fine," Ezra said.

The detective waited until he shut the door.

"I've told him—"

"I've been trying to reach you for days," Detective Martinez said. Her scowl was unfamiliar to me. "Carlos Garcia died. He never regained consciousness."

This hit me hard. I had to sit down. I thought about the bald man with his gloved hands pushing against the older man's chest—Garcia flailing, falling. It had looked like murder and now it was murder. Only fifteen days had gone by, but hearing about Garcia's death was like learning someone I'd known for the better part of my life was gone.

"Also there's this," Detective Martinez said. "Carlos Garcia was A. Craig."

"What? Wait, what do you mean?"

"*A. Craig* is an anagram for *Garcia*."

I had forgotten A. Craig was a pseudonym.

"How do you know it's him?" I asked.

"We were in—or I should say Allagash's crew was in Garcia's apartment and accessed his laptop. They found the original article and all of the drafts. Also some notes for another essay he never finished."

"About what?" I asked.

"About how none of this, the whole stranger game, none of it was what he hoped to inspire."

So he was deliberately disrupting the staging in the way the two tourists thought he was.

"Allagash told you this?" I asked.

"I have my sources," Detective Martinez said.

"What else did the essay say?" I asked.

She didn't answer me. She asked, "What's going on? Why is he here?"

How was this any of her concern?

"I don't think it's a good idea for you to be spending time with him right now," she said.

I was baffled. I must have looked baffled.

I didn't exactly see myself reconciling with Ezra, but I became defensive and said, "You know how it goes. You and your husband got back together, right?"

Detective Martinez appeared confused: What was I talking about, her husband? Which made me wonder if she even had a husband. My trust in her was evaporating, and I made the decision not to tell her about seeing Carey with the bald guy.

"Listen, Rebecca," she said, "I don't think you grasp the gravity of the situation. Allagash is now running a murder investigation."

"And I'm a suspect?"

"You need to be very careful where you go and what you do and who you're with—"

"Are the police on the take?" I asked. I surprised myself by blurting this out. "With the stranger game. Helping players, stagers. Trespassers."

"Is that something Ezra told you?" Martinez asked back.

Before I could put my question to her again, she touched her ear—I hadn't realized she was wearing an earpiece—and said, "Martinez, go ahead." Then she sighed. "I guess it really was only a matter of time. I'm nearby." And to me: "I need to go."

"What happened?"

She hesitated but told me: two players breaking into the home of a stranger they were following had been ambushed and shot by the stranger, whom Detective Martinez speculated had faked his departure only to return right away.

"And the players who got shot?" I asked.

"One dead, I don't know about the other," she said, and then she left.

I was paranoid now about my house being bugged and made Ezra come outside so I could fill him in. Even then, I whispered. I had been so thrown off by Detective Martinez's revelations that I hadn't asked her anything about trespassers or how the police might be involved in the game. Ezra repeated his mistrust of her. There was something essential, something significant the detective wasn't revealing, and I couldn't say why—it was only a premonition—but I worried he might be right. I wanted to be alone to think.

I said, "Thanks for coming over yesterday and again today."

Ezra didn't move.

"I'll talk to you later," I said.

"I got you into this," he said, "and I will see you safely out of it."

"You don't need—"

"Don't worry. After this is over I will disappear again, and you can go back to not worrying about wanting what you want. Or whatever you said."

I didn't have the energy to fight him. I kept picturing Garcia broken against the rocks and felt defeated anew.

IT WAS MUCH LATER THAT I READ THE NOTES FOR THE essay that Carlos Garcia never finished and which mysteriously ended up on the internet.

(1) When I was young and striking out, I believed that my legacy would be a series of scholarly books and articles that advanced the understanding of a time and place and which with any luck would direct the discourse for the generation that followed. But now I see that the things you leave behind are not very important; what is important is how you positively and affirmatively affect the people in your life. My students, my lovers perhaps, my colleagues, my friends. All the new people I met in my new life and maybe only knew for a day or two. For as long as these people were alive, they would carry me in their minds and hearts; after they

were gone, they themselves would be carried in the minds and hearts of those whom they touched, and so on.

But what a dark stone it is in my chest to know that I have adversely affected countless strangers who have looked at this thing I left behind and misread it and misused it, folding it inside out, this unknown, unseen, thrill-seeking, anarchic mob that wreaks discord and distrust, that sows despair.

If I had known any of this would happen, I would have kept my story to myself.

(2) I stayed away much longer than I would have predicted, resigning my position at the university in order to work as a night manager at the desert inn, eventually becoming the day manager and volunteer tour guide. I made the coffee in the morning and set out the breakfast buffet. I drew arrows on maps. I chatted with the guests who came and went, playing board games with them in the afternoon, sometimes sharing whiskey with them at night. They were the transients; I was the fixture. This suited me. And my folly was ignoring any and all news from the city.

One day guests who were traveling across country told me about being in the city with friends. They went on a hike. There was some kind of scene they witnessed, two people arguing, becoming physical. Someone in their group wanted to call the police, and someone else decided to intervene right then. I wasn't sure why it was important for the guests at the inn to tell me about this until they explained it was all a hoax, the argument and the fight put on just for them, all paid for by their hosts, likely a tidy sum for it, although the guests only found out about this by accident later when the hosts had been drinking.

I was lost, and so they explained they were playing the stranger game, and I had to ask what was the stranger game, and then try to understand its scope, and how any of it got started. Once illuminated, I had to excuse myself and went into the office and started to look the whole thing up. I could barely breathe.

I do not recall another moment in my life when I have felt as fevered with shame.

(3) Denial that this whole phenomenon was born from my essay. Then anger, et cetera. Then accepting this to be the case. More research, the same cycle of feelings. Utter bewilderment, utter disdain.

Would someone else in my position be amused? Not care? Say, oh, well, and continue living life as life was being lived?

(4) I could not remain idle, so I returned to the city. First I needed to survey what was going on. Then figure out how to stop it. Intervene. Interfere.

But how exactly?

When you never intended to be any kind of prophet and when you have lost complete control over what your words mean, how do you get people to listen to you?

WE BECAME TRESPASSERS. THIS WAS EZRA'S SCHEME for how we would get inside information on the game, although I wasn't clear what we were going to do with what we gleaned: Blackmail the police into permanently leaving me alone? It was a ridiculous gambit, not to mention risky given the report of a subject ambushing his followers. The only reason I did the driving the next morning was out of fear Ezra would do something truly stupid if left on his own.

We cruised along the boulevard a ways before Ezra pointed out a woman exiting a children's clothing store. She packed a bunch of small shopping bags in her trunk. We followed her to the grocery store. We waited in the lot and followed her up into the hills. We parked across the street from her ranch house.

"Now she has to go pick up from school whoever the clothing was purchased for," Ezra reasoned.

"If you want to prowl around someone's house, why can't we just do that? Why do we have to go through the whole rigmarole of a random follow?" I asked, not for the first time.

"You know why. You know how the game is played," Ezra said.

"We also don't know whether anyone else is home," I said.

"Perfect," Ezra said.

After the better part of an hour sitting in my car, I was ready to leave, but then the woman emerged, looking like she was headed to the gym. As soon as she drove off, we walked across the street and then around to the back, which was an unfenced slope of brush a lot like my place. Seeing the same kind of patio with the same clay pots of ill-tended plants, the same open view of the city basin—and thinking now that like me this woman lived alone (who was to say for whom she'd purchased the children's outfits?)—I myself felt vulnerable and by association violated. I wanted to turn around. Ezra, however, was checking sliding glass doors and windows to see if any would open. He cupped his hands around his eyes to peer inside. I stood back, the lookout, although Ezra wanted us to get caught.

"Someone is putting together a jigsaw puzzle on the dining table," he said. "The borders are done."

"Ezra, I don't like this. Let's go," I said.

"No, wait," he said.

"No one is going to report us. No one can see or hear us back here the way this house is sited."

I decided to go home with or without Ezra, but he did come with me, and back in the car insisted we try again. I said no, that was enough; Ezra said he'd continue without me; I told him to go ahead, but then I neither dropped him off nor relinquished my car keys.

The weather was wearing me down: the wind rushing in from the east shrouded the sky in a jaundiced scrim. Everybody knew crime rates went up when the air became this dusty and motionless and hot. Our recklessness almost seemed sanctioned.

We followed a man picking up two young kids from a dance studio, but after pursuing his minivan awhile and after watching the man, presumably the father, swing by a playground and retrieve more children, we decided instead to track a woman also collecting young kids. She drove along residential streets to a house, where she and the children all filed inside. We waited, but it didn't appear anyone was going to come out again.

Back on the boulevard, we tracked a man moving through errands, the dry cleaners, the hardware store, but he didn't head up into a neighborhood. He parked in front of a café, where he sat at a sidewalk table and was joined by a woman whose parted curtain of long hair and round sunglasses made it difficult to measure whether for her part what appeared to be a date was going well. I said it was a date: the man's posture was stiff at first, straight, but then he leaned in, he was laughing at something, shaking his head oh, my. Ezra read them as old friends who hadn't seen each other for a long time. In any case, they lingered, and I didn't find them terribly fascinating, but we kept on watching.

"It's Monday," I said. "Don't these people have jobs?"

I was one to talk. Ezra ignored me.

Eventually they paid their bill and the man got back in his car, the woman in hers a few spots away. He pulled out into the street slowly, waited for her, and she followed him. We trailed them up into a nearby neighborhood, and while the man pulled into a driveway, the woman remained parked on the street, the engine running. The man dashed in the house with his dry cleaning and then popped out again moments later. He got in the woman's car, and then they were gone.

One more time we went around to the rear of the house; the properties were narrower on this street, the neighbors closer. I was surprised to find a neat rectangular pool occupying most of a flat backyard. The house was all wood vertical siding in front, but glass in back. We could see the master bedroom, the unmade bed; the television over the living room fireplace was twice the size of the hearth.

Ezra kicked off his shoes, tugged off his socks. I was afraid he'd shrug off his jeans next—he did.

"You're kidding," I said.

"It's like when you saw the trespassers the first time," he said and with his back to me pulled off his shirt.

"The only time," I said. "Wait, keep your—"

Too late. He stepped out of his boxer briefs. I tried not to look at him. I looked at him. He dove neatly into the deep end and disappeared underwater. I watched him swim a slow lap, the water sliding off his back and butt. It was difficult not to stare, to see him naked like this, to think about the last time we were intimate, what happened after that.

Ezra had always been so at ease with his body in a way I wasn't. It was an early gift, the way he made me comfortable around him, appreciated, sexual. I would have to say after we split up, I'd lost that unselfconsciousness being around other naked bodies. I waited until he was swimming away from me before hastily stepping out of my jeans and throwing off my top. I climbed down the ladder into the pool. My underwear clung to my body, revealed everything anyway. I reasoned that if the man returned home with his date or if the police did come, I would preserve some modesty. Or maybe I tricked myself into believing that technically I wasn't completely naked with Ezra, but why was I in the water at all?

I remained submerged up to my neck in the deep end while Ezra kept swimming. The pool was lined with dark stucco, making the water dark, too; our bodies by contrast appeared to glow. Ezra's farmer's tan made him look like he was wearing long gloves. Even as an adoles-

cent I had never done anything like this, but I knew Ezra
had. For a moment I forgot why we were doing what we
were doing and simply felt—what? Young.

Ezra swam over to me and slapped his hands against
the surface.

"Hey," I said. "Be nice."

He wanted to make noise and splashed more water, but
why would the neighbors suspect that we were trespassers? The splashing could be coming from the man who
lived here or his guests, us in this case, friends given access on a warm day near the solstice.

When I came back up for air Ezra was close to me.
The waves we made bobbed up against the coping. He
seemed sober to me now, like something serious needed
to be said. I didn't want to hear it, so I swam over quickly
to the ladder in an efficient freestyle and got out. How
foolish I felt putting my clothes back on without towel-
ing off, my clothes immediately soaked through.

"We can dry off first in the sun," Ezra said from the
pool.

Barefoot, I headed back through the gate and out to
the front. I'd forgotten my shoes, but Ezra appeared moments later with them. His drenched shirt and pants
clung to his narrow frame.

At my house I threw our clothes in the dryer, and we
took turns in the bathroom, and while Ezra was in the
shower, I did something I shouldn't have done and never
had done while we were together. Ezra had kept a jour-

nal since he was a teenager, and I knew I would find his
current one in his shoulder bag, which I did. I wasn't
sure what I was looking for, maybe simply an entry that
might reveal what he'd been thinking about since returning to the city. I didn't read anything though because in
quickly flipping pages, I noticed sketches instead—he'd
said a colony resident had taught him some drawing ba-
sics. There were rough outlines of elderly oaks. And he
said he'd been drawing from memory—he had. I found
pages of very linear but very accurate drawings of me.
Me in an armchair reading a book. Me staring out the
window. Me looking at him (presumably), my hair longer than it was now. I didn't think anyone but me would
recognize myself—technically he wasn't that sharp. But
that wasn't the point. He'd said I'd been in his thoughts,
and here was proof. I slid the journal back into his bag
when I heard him turn off the shower.

Ezra borrowed a hotel robe, which fit him fine. We
didn't say much. I wanted to open a bottle of white wine,
which made me remember the one time (the only time)
we'd committed a crime together in the past, a misde-
meanor. I had to dig around in the back of a kitchen
drawer but found the waiter's corkscrew we'd lifted, that
I'd plucked from a bin and slid into Ezra's jacket pocket:
it had a red handle embellished with a gold fleur-de-lis,
the fleur-de-lis mostly worn away. I showed it to Ezra,
who didn't recognize it at first. Then he grinned.

"You still have that, wow," he said. "That's from one of those early drives up the coast."

"We brought a bottle from home but forgot the cork-screw, classic, and we were in that town, in that knick-knack-gewgaw-gadget shop, but I guess we'd left our wallets—"

"Oh, we had the cash," Ezra said. "It was more for the thrill that you took it. You looked at me and winked and grabbed it."

"But it was in your coat when we left the store," I said.

"True," Ezra said. "We were thieves together."

"So wild."

I wondered if his memory of that road trip matched mine. The high bed at the inn, the fraying quilts. The noisy ocean, the salt in the air. This was long ago now. Aging suddenly seemed unfair.

We drank the bottle of wine, had scrambled eggs for dinner, drank half of another bottle. Ezra was renting a room near where his apartment had been, but the wine had made him too groggy to drive, and I told him to stay. So as not to be ambiguous, I threw two pillows and a blanket on the couch. From my bedroom, I tried to listen to him breathing, but all I heard was wind in the scrub, knocking around chimes blocks away. I slept poorly, barely slept at all.

I pictured the bald guy bringing his hands up in the air, setting them squarely against Garcia's chest and Garcia's expression when he realized he was falling back—the roundness of his brow, of his mouth: Why?

In the morning I had to ask, "Is this about justice for you, about Garcia's death? Or is it more about getting back at Carey?"

"Both. Neither," Ezra said. "I don't know."

The way he was looking at me then, or rather not looking at me and instead staring at the floor, pained, apologetic, I suspected what he wanted most was to make everything right by me.

"We could call the police on ourselves," I said.

"We cannot report our own trespassing."

"Why not?"

"We have to look like the real deal," Ezra said, "or we won't find out anything."

"Fine," I said, but I set new terms: we could claim we were playing the stranger game, but no more actual random follows. No more chance.

We set out on foot on a street that wound down from my house, and it didn't take long to latch on to a morning dog walker. Although we were technically still in my neighborhood, I knew neither the slender man fixated on his cell phone nor his slender hound, who stopped every five feet to sniff the ground. Maybe the dog truly was interested in all of the trash cans, car tires, and dewy weeds he needed to smell, but equally likely, he wanted to forestall the inevitable: being left alone for the day. The man tugged the dog along at a certain point and picked up the pace. He wasn't inside his house for long before he left again, briefcase in hand, and drove away.

We hoped the dog would see us around back and bark. No such luck: he paced back and forth along sliding glass doors and whimpered and wagged his tail when we tried to open it. Freedom wasn't coming, sorry, dog. The patio had a built-in barbecue, its lid thrown back. We could start a fire on the grill, send up smoke signals. Ezra lay back on a wicker chaise and looked amused watching me bounce around looking for an alarm we could set off, but to do that, we'd probably need to break a window and get inside. My insomnia had left me a little delirious: I was on my knees trying to find a stone in the shallow herb garden to hurl, but then the thought of the broken glass and the dog padding around gave me pause. Ezra was giggling. This went on awhile.

"What's so funny?" I asked.

"You should see yourself. You—"

When he stopped midsentence and sprang up, I looked where he was looking: two police officers were standing by the gate, each with his right hand hovering over his holster. We would never learn if the neighbors spotted us and called, or if the homeowner returned and saw us, or if someone else had been in the house.

I was standing, hands in the air. So was Ezra, although no guns were drawn and neither officer had instructed us to assume this posture, so in effect we were professing our guilt unprompted.

"Mind telling us what's going on?" one officer asked.

I started to answer: "We thought…" I was nervous.

"You thought what?" the second officer asked.

When Ezra lowered his hands, the first officer said, "That's okay. Why don't you keep them up for us."

This cop looked familiar; it was possible he'd been part of the crew removing Carey's belongings from my house.

"We're players," Ezra said. "We heard—"

"That there's protection," I said.

The officers glanced at each other.

"We don't know what you're referring to," the first officer said.

I put my arms down, and so did Ezra. Neither officer told us to put them back up. I tried to bluff my way through this: we were only trying to take the stranger game to the next level, and this was something we'd heard rumors about. Were we mistaken that the police were not opposed to this kind of recreation so long as no property was damaged and no one was hurt in the process?

The first officer nodded at the second officer, who stepped back through the gate toward the street.

"Did you hire a tour guide?" the officer asked.

"A tour guide," Ezra said.

"You have to clear it first," the officer said. "And pay the fees."

"Oh," I said. "That makes sense. We're so sorry. We didn't know."

"How much usually is it?" Ezra asked.

The officer said all costs and such were set by the tour guide. We'd have to speak to one directly.

"Right now you'll need to leave," he said and opened the gate. "We can let this go. Next time, make arrangements first."

Ezra and I walked in front of the officer out to the street, where the other officer was smoking a cigarette.

"How do we find a tour guide?" Ezra asked.

Again the two officers exchanged glances. The second one chuckled, and the first officer shook his head and laughed at something, too. He pulled out a citation pad, ripped off a blank ticket, and wrote an address on the back.

"The rest is up to you," he said.

"You followed by car?" the second officer asked.

"We walked," I said.

"Then I suggest you walk away now," he said.

Back at my house, Ezra located the address of the so-called tour guide on his phone map.

"Can we take a moment before we get in much deeper?" I asked. "We've established that the police are corrupt. Isn't that a big deal?"

"We already knew that," he said. "Come on."

He was heading for his car this time, not mine, and he drove. I wondered how many tour guides there were; I suspected the network was vast. I also wondered if this was a trap.

"Why would it be a trap?" Ezra asked.

"Bribery has to be worse than trespassing," I said. "This would be a bigger collar."

"Collar," Ezra said. "The words you use now."

"Don't be mean to me," I said. We both were worn out and cross.

It didn't take long to find the house in the flats south of where I lived and on the other side of the boulevard. I had been on this street before, this block, in fact.

"There it is," Ezra said.

He had pulled opposite a small house, a cottage painted green, the trim a darker green.

"Oh, no," I said and slid down in my seat. "That's the address? You're sure?"

"It's what the officer wrote down," Ezra said. "Should we knock?"

"No," I said, *"no,"* and tugged at Ezra's sleeve so he'd slide down in his seat, too. "I've been here before."

"You have?"

"We have to get out of here."

"But—"

"Ezra, drive away. Now. Please."

"I don't—"

"Please," I pleaded, and he shifted the car in gear and continued down the block, then doubled back along a parallel street.

We sat in his car outside my house. He waited. I was massaging my temples with my fingers.

"Do you want to tell me who lives in that house?" he asked.

"Detective Martinez," I said, and I could not have been more spun around.

ALL TRUST WAS GONE, TRUST WAS ANTIQUATED, TRUST quaint. Betrayal was routine, betrayal was sport. I vowed never again to allow myself to be so deceived.

I claimed I was going to lie down and closed the door to my bedroom, but sat in a chair in the corner and watched the dance of afternoon light across the spines of books packed into tall shelves. I could hear Ezra puttering in the other room. He left me alone. When I opened the door later, it turned out he had been putting away dishes, taking out the trash, sweeping.

"You don't need to do that," I said. What I meant was: I can take care of myself.

"Are you okay?" Ezra asked.

"I'm fine," I said. And then: "We are never going to figure this out."

"But Martinez, Allagash—"

"I'm convinced they're working together. They're all in cahoots."

"Cahoots," Ezra said.

"Stop making fun of the words I use," I snapped.

"I meant *cahoots* sounds too cute," he said.

"Anyway I'm done," I said.

"What do you mean done?"

"This has gotten too risky."

Ezra stared at me.

"I'm sorry, but you really don't sound like yourself," he said.

"I don't even know what that means. I'm done trying to figure out the stranger game network and the connection to the police or why Garcia would be pushed to his death."

"I don't believe you," Ezra said. "You don't like unsolved puzzles—"

"Puzzles? *Puzzles* is what sounds too cute," I said. "While I was in the bedroom, I decided to go into the office tomorrow. I've been gone long enough."

"Really," Ezra said.

"I talked to Rick the other day, and he said that if I'm in better shape, he thinks I should return. Everyone agrees."

"I don't believe you," Ezra said again.

"So you keep saying. I'm out of cash and I need to go back to work." This was almost true. Then I added, "And I'm sure you need to find a job, too."

Ezra was at a loss.

"I need to get ready for tomorrow," I said.

He didn't move.

"Alone," I said.

"I'll call you later."

"You don't need to."

"Tomorrow—"

"No need."

"When can I see you?" he asked.

I didn't answer him, so he stepped forward and drew me into a defiant hug. I didn't embrace him with the same passion. My hands rested on his shoulder blades. He didn't let go. My hands slid down to his middle back, two ridges, a straight river running through the dell between. His breath warmed my neck. He let go first.

LYING AWAKE THAT NIGHT, WHAT I FIXATED ON WAS
how long it had been since I had exerted any sort of control in my own life. I needed to take charge, although
I knew Ezra was right: I didn't sound like myself, and
by extension I wasn't behaving like myself either. Some
bolder truculent version of me was at the wheel the next
morning when I drove up to the police station near the
park and told the sergeant at the front desk I wanted to
speak with Detective Allagash.

The sergeant gave me a once-over. "And you are?"
she asked.

There was something about her narrow face—I'd seen
her before, but out of uniform. How did I know her?

I gave my name and said, "He's expecting me," because in a way I thought he was.

I didn't recognize Detective Allagash at first because
he'd shaved his mustache. His face looked so blank, like

a sundial at noon. He ushered me into the same room where I'd been brought seventeen days earlier.

"I'm surprised to see you," he said, jovial, like we were old pals. "How have you been? How can I help you today?"

He threw me off by being so affable.

"I'm wondering why haven't you questioned me again," I said.

Detective Allagash feigned surprise. "Questioned you?"

"You said you would be wanting to talk to me again."

The detective stroked his upper lip, maybe not yet used to having no hair there.

"Is there something in particular you'd like to tell me?" he asked.

"No," I said. "But when you were at my house— Am I under investigation for murder?"

I couldn't tell whether the detective was amused or confused.

"Would you like to amend your statement? Is that why you're here?" he asked.

"No," I said. "I was under the impression that you were investigating me."

He leaned in. "And why do you think that? Who told you that?"

The detective himself had instructed me not to leave town without telling him: it had certainly sounded like a threat.

"Never mind," he said. "I am pretty sure I know who gave you that idea."

"What about Carey?" I asked.

"I can't really comment on an open case."

"What about the bald guy?"

"Who?" the detective asked—he was playing me. "As I said, I can't comment. But I will say it's been several weeks since the event, and as you might imagine, the longer we're out there, the colder the trail gets."

This was his way of telling me they were burying the case, wasn't it? I was certain now that he was involved with the tour guides, with who knew what else, and for whatever reason, he didn't want Carey connected to what had happened to Garcia, and all trace of Carey had been erased.

"Can I make a suggestion, Ms. Crane? Why don't you go home and try to move on? You need to accept that we don't always solve every crime. Why don't you go home and get on with your life?"

"I'm not sure I can," I said.

"Try," Detective Allagash said, glaring at me, and he did not look so amiable now.

I didn't know what I had expected to discover, and on the way out, I studied the sergeant behind the front desk. She looked up, then back at her monitor—oh, no. I recognized her now: she was the stager who worked with the bald guy, the first time wearing a wig, the second time with her hair in a ponytail the way it was now. And she was a cop, too?

I was a little shaky, but my next move had to be to confront Detective Martinez. I drove to her precinct house. Here the officer at the counter told me that the detective wasn't in today. When I asked when she'd return, the officer said that wasn't information he could share.

"Then I'll drive over to her place and see if she's there," I said, except I hadn't meant to say this aloud, and the officer asked for my name before I left.

I was probably lucky a squad car didn't trail me when I drove to the detective's house, where no cars were parked in the driveway, and from which no dogs could be heard barking when I knocked on the door. I wasn't about to give up and decided to cruise the neighborhood, rehearsing what I'd say when I found her, that I knew she'd only pretended to be my ally, that she was just as corrupt as every other cop on the force. I headed over to the hardware store where I'd once run into her, but she didn't emerge. This was ludicrous—*I* was ludicrous. Did I really think I could express anything to her other than how confused I was? After the hardware store, I wove in and out of blocks for an hour with no real strategy. Eventually it occurred to me where I should go, and I curved around the reservoir past the dog park where, lo and behold, I spotted the detective wrangling her two big wooly dogs. It appeared she was trying to separate them from a retriever in whom they'd both taken an interest.

Even from across the street, I could hear Detective Martinez yelling, "You stop, you stop."

She was out of uniform but wearing police-issued sweats and T-shirt. Eventually she guided both dogs into the back of her square sedan, which I guess she drove around even off duty. I knew that Detective Martinez of all people was probably especially good at knowing when she was being followed, so I hung back several cars behind her on the boulevard to avoid detection.

Ten minutes later, she turned a corner and glided into her driveway. Right as I was about to turn onto her street, too, I noticed a white car parked in front of her house, so I pulled over. I had a good angle on the detective's front door, however, and I could watch her let her two dogs inside, only to turn around to face someone shouting that he wanted a word with her. It was Ezra, Ezra getting out of his car and heading up her front path. Of course he and I had the same rough plan to confront her.

Because the detective was holding open her front door, her dogs poured down the stoop again and simultaneously peed on the browned-out lawn. The detective snapped her fingers twice and they obediently trotted back inside. She did not ask Ezra in.

I could watch but not hear them. Ezra's gestures were large, his hands going up in the air at one point as if he

were throwing confetti. The detective was letting him
rant but shaking her head from side to side in disagree-
ment. It was hard to tell, but I thought that even she
was going to lose her cool. Then she scratched her head
and, it looked like, asked Ezra a series of questions, to
which he didn't react well: he was shrugging, throwing
his hands up in the air again, exasperated, and when he
jabbed his finger toward her chest, she grabbed his hand
and held it in front of her a moment like a captured spi-
der she wasn't sure she should release or kill. She said
something that Ezra didn't like the sound of—I noted
the way his shoulders sloped—and when the detective
released his hand, he let it fall to his side. She went inside and shut the door.

Ezra didn't step off her stoop at first. When he did
walk back to his car, I ducked low—I didn't think he saw
me. He leaned forward and rested his head against the
steering wheel. He turned the ignition, which I took as
my cue to execute a swift U-turn and drive away.

My foray had been pointless. I'd determined nothing, and if I wanted to know what Ezra had found out,
I'd have to reach out to him, which I wasn't going to
do. Sitting at a stoplight, I screamed in frustration. Now
what—*now what*!

I arrived home to find a handwritten note tucked into
a small white envelope and taped to my front door. It
had to have been left after I'd gone out, deliberately left
while I wasn't home, I decided, which meant I was being

watched. I read it several times in my kitchen before leaving it on my counter and stepping back cautiously as if it were a stunned animal, which once reoriented would leap up and snap at me.

Dear Rebecca,

I know you must be wondering where I've been. I had to go into hiding. I am about to leave town for good, never to return. But before I go, I want to apologize to you and explain what has been going on. Maybe this is selfish of me, but I need that closure. Maybe you do, too.

I fell in love with you, and this is not the way I wanted things to turn out. Please let me say how sorry I am in person.

Will you meet me tomorrow at noon at the abandoned house up in the canyon? I know you probably don't want to hike back up there, but I think it's safe because it's the last place anyone would expect us to go. I trust you to come alone.

You have no idea how much I've missed you. I doubt I can make things right, but I want to try. Please let me try.

Love,
Carey

I DIDN'T HAVE ANY OTHER NOTES OR GROCERY LISTS lying around to verify it was Carey's handwriting, but I believed it was. I couldn't remember him ever saying he loved me before. I wasn't moved—was this a trap? I also could not deny that the prospect of an explanation appealed to me a great deal, his contrition. And then I replayed the pantomime exchange I'd witnessed on Detective Martinez's stoop: What exactly was Ezra up to? These men who disappeared on me and returned when it suited them, rueful, penitent—why should I have faith in either of them?

At some point, I lay down to rest my eyes for a few minutes—and awoke in darkness hours later, disoriented, the day a riddle. I thought I heard footsteps out on my terrace and bolted up. In the kitchen I turned on all of the outside lights. No one was there.

I reread Carey's note on the counter where I'd left it,

curling now in the hot night. There was no way I could meet him on these terms.

I tried and failed to go back to sleep, made a sandwich at three in the morning, and decided it was my turn to disappear without a trace. I packed a bag with a week's worth of clothing and a backpack with all of the books on my night table. I showered and waited for sunrise, when I would vanish.

Sitting in the corner chair in my bedroom, I didn't nod off, but I wasn't fully awake either. I thought about that first clean crosscourt forehand I hit with Carey's spare racket when I found him practicing his serve. Handing him produce at the farmer's market to place in our bag, zucchini, mushrooms, parsnip, thyme. We had fallen asleep the same way every night with Carey behind me, surrounding me, although as the weather became warmer, I would wiggle free after his breathing slowed and he was out, and then in the middle of the night, I'd wake up and he would have inched over to me and embraced me again, like he needed me in order to sleep. He could not have been acting the entire time. There had to have been a turn, and this was what I most wanted to know: When was the turn?

I would like to blame the weather, the deadening heat that shadowless morning—and maybe the sun did in some way exacerbate my loneliness and impair my ability to reason—but I can't claim I didn't fathom the risks. Here in front of me was a trial, and arrogantly I believed

I could get through it and be stronger, and then break back into being who I wanted to be in life. I don't know that I will ever be able to explain why instead of tossing my bag and backpack in my trunk and driving out of the city, I calculated how long I would need to drive up to the park and hike up to the abandoned house in order to arrive precisely at noon.

There were a few cars in the parking lot; none that I recognized. No one was out playing tennis, nor hiking for that matter; no one was ahead of me on the trail, the sun too white. I didn't think to bring a water bottle or a hat. I heard footsteps again, behind me now, and I looked around (I kept looking around the entire way), but I was only hearing the crunch of dry grass beneath my own boots.

I picked up the pace. Maybe I could get there first— yes, I should have worked it out to get there first. Say what you have to say, and then I never want to see you again. Say what you have to say, and then I want to have crazy, crazy sex right here in this empty house, and then I never want to see you again. Say what you have to say, and then I want you to drive with me out of the city, no conversation, no destination—everyone dreams of living an improvised life, let's do it.

A new padlock had been inserted into the warped fence, making it impossible to shimmy through. Police tape had been wound around the gate, as well. I climbed it and straddled it briefly before landing hard on the other side. I didn't want to go back through the house, so I took the exterior stairs down to the terrace.

And there he was.

Unshaven, his hair a mess. Wasn't he too warm wearing a hoodie and jeans? He was standing at the edge of the terrace with its unfinished wall. I stood at the bottom of the stairs, one foot on the bottom step, half arriving, half exiting.

"You came after all," he said. "I wasn't sure you would."

When I pictured Garcia falling right where Carey was now standing, I thought I might faint.

"Are you alone?" he asked.

"I am," I said. "Hello."

"Hi. Can you come closer?" he asked, but I didn't move. "Please?"

I took two steps forward: say what you have to say.

"Oh, Rebecca. I'm so very sorry."

He pushed up his sleeves. His hoodie was half soaked through with sweat.

"Can you come closer? I don't want to shout."

I took another step toward him, only one.

"I want you to know that I really did—do—love you, Rebecca. We were so happy."

Was that true? I started to ask my question: "When exactly—?"

"I told you about how I owed a lot of money. That

pressure was always there," Carey said. "I'd been in touch
with someone back when I was playing the game—"

"The bald guy?"

"Yes."

"What is his name?" I asked.

"It's better you don't know. I'm telling you all of this so
you don't have to walk around trying to figure out what
happened, but then you should forget about all of it—"

"Is Carey *your* real name?" I asked.

"You know it is! Why? Did someone tell you otherwise?"

"Various detectives," I said.

"Oh, well, they would I guess," Carey said.

"They would? Why?"

"Can you come a little closer? Please?"

I did move in, but not all the way next to him.

"You owed money," I said. "You were trying to figure out a way to pay off your debt."

Carey nodded. "Sometimes when you were at your
office," he said, "I worked as a stager."

He stepped closer to me.

"Oh," I said. "Did you work for the bald guy—"

"Yes."

"Were the police—"

"You don't need to know. It's so much better if you
don't know."

This irked me. "I came here because you said you
would explain everything."

"I did, I know. Let me try."

"Maybe I don't need to know," I said, because oddly at that moment I was satisfied.

He'd been playing the game, followed me, hurt me, apologized, fallen for me, been with me, wanted to be with me, but his debts were too great, he was in too deep. All of this I could believe, all of this made sense. I started to turn around to leave and Carey lurched forward and grabbed my arm. He immediately let go.

"I'm sorry," he said. "But please don't go yet. Please."

We were standing next to each other now near the edge of the terrace, close enough for me to see how the sun evinced his freckles.

"What really happened that morning when we hiked up here?" I asked. "What was really going on?"

"As I said, I worked for...for the man you refer to as the bald guy," Carey said.

"Right, you said, but what about that morning? You wanted to go on a hike—"

"Alone. You weren't supposed to come. I got a call that there was someone disrupting stagings and my help was needed to distract him and stop him. I was given the time and place where they expected he'd be."

"He was set up," I said. "Why did you agree to let me come with you?"

Carey shrugged. "I don't know exactly. I thought it would be fun for you to see another staging? Or maybe I thought I'd distract this guy, this staging disruptor—"

"Carlos Garcia," I said.

"Yes. And then this would give me the opportunity to come clean about everything. I wouldn't have to hide anything anymore."

This seemed believable to me, but: "Did you know that Garcia was A. Craig?"

Carey nodded. "They didn't want him to mess with the game anymore. It was no longer his. He needed to let it go."

They sounded ominous. Who was *they*? Or maybe I should ask: How vast was *they*?

"It never really was his game," I said. "Did you know that the bald guy was going to push him—"

"No!" Carey said. "I definitely wasn't told that would happen. And I don't know if it happened in part because we were late—"

"We were?"

"We stopped to talk to the police about your neighbor's burglary, and by the time we got up here…" His voice had grown quieter, as if he was worried about being overheard even with no one around us.

"It was an accident?" I asked.

"They told me we'd only rough him up."

I couldn't follow this. "Who is *they* and who is *we*?"

"Does that really matter? You have to believe me. Do you believe me?"

I did and I didn't.

"Why was the bald guy wearing surgical gloves?" I

asked, because maybe he hadn't intended to kill Garcia, but he did plan on causing him grave harm and didn't want to leave a trace.

Carey stared at me, his eyes darting left to right, left to right. What did this detail mean to me? Where was I going with this inquiry?

"I didn't think they would push him. You have to believe me," he said again.

"But they did."

Then there was Allagash removing Carey's things from my place, pushing his investigation, threatening me, but then when I saw him again, he was all lackadaisical about the prospects of closing a murder case. Maybe he wanted to erase any connection between the bald guy and Carey. Carey was either lying to me or didn't understand with whom he was involved. Unless—

"I wish we could go back in time, Rebecca. I wish I could wake up next to you again."

Unless the reason Carey was summoned to the abandoned house wasn't to help stop Garcia from shooing away players or to scare Garcia off from reasserting his moral sway with another essay. Perhaps *they* wanted Carey at the house so he could witness what they were capable of doing to people like him who didn't pay off debts, who didn't fall into line and do their bidding. Carey knew too much. Maybe he'd stopped playing along; maybe he'd gone rogue. They lured Garcia to the house by setting up a staging for him to interfere with the way he had been lately (and he must have been having some success). They gave Carey a reason he didn't fully understand to make sure he was up here at the same time so they could threaten him indirectly. But what did it mean that I witnessed everything, as well, when that wasn't part of the original plan? Who now was *I* to *them*?

Carey tucked a loose strand of my hair back behind my ear. I flinched.

He had stepped forward without my realizing it, close enough to whisper, "I only want to hold you again. Can we hold each other?"

His breath smelled like vinegar.

He said, "I knew you'd see me at the sculpture garden. I knew you'd come by the tennis court that afternoon. Then it would all be wonderful after that."

His voice sounded exactly the way it did the first night at my house, unctuous, creepy. Your sweater. You didn't see me, you never saw me? Maybe then I do win.

Here he was, who he had been all along.

"I thought you had to go into hiding," I said. "That's what you said in your note."

"I did. I do."

He leaned in to kiss me. I leaned back.

"Then why were you out in the open meeting with the bald guy at a sidewalk café?" I asked.

Carey straightened his back. He started to say something and didn't.

"You were in public—"

"So nothing would happen," Carey said. "Nothing would happen at a café with everybody watching."

He was afraid. He had been successfully intimidated.

"What were you arguing about?" I asked.

Carey grabbed my forearm again, this time not letting go. It was not affectionate. He gripped it tighter and tugged me toward him. When I tried to pull away, he held on.

"What were we arguing about? Well," he said, "I said I had a lot of information he probably didn't want widely known, but he didn't exactly like being put in that position. And so he turned it around on me. He said, 'If you fix things, then we'll wipe the slate clean.'"

"Let go," I said.

My wrist was throbbing. He was speaking in abstractions and clichés, and I didn't know what he meant. Or maybe I did. If you fix things.

"I wasn't supposed to bring you that morning, but I did," Carey said, "and Allagash, oh, he wasn't too pleased about that."

"Let. Go."

"But I told him not to worry. I convinced him you wouldn't be a problem."

The more I tried to wriggle free, the tighter Carey's grip. It felt like he could snap my wrist.

"But you had to go to him yesterday, didn't you," he said. "Now look where we are."

As I tried to pull away again, my feet were slipping on the dry, dirty slate—

"Rebecca?"

This call echoed from inside the empty house. Both Carey and I pivoted. Ezra emerged onto the terrace.

"What's going on?" he asked, approaching us fast. "Let go of her," he said.

Which Carey did, and he took a step away from me, reached around toward the small of his back, and pulled out a stubby black gun from his belt. It looked like a toy in his long fingers, like all he could do with it was start a race. Carey pointed the gun at Ezra, and Ezra stopped halfway across the terrace.

I had left Carey's note on my kitchen counter. Ezra must have let himself in and found it there—but he wouldn't have let himself in unless he worried something was very wrong.

"I told you to come alone," Carey said.

He let his arm fall briefly to his side, and Ezra stepped closer. Carey aimed the gun again. Ezra stood still.

Now the sun was a heavy cloth dropping over all of us, pressing down against us. I knew then with certainty that Carey's motives were malevolent and that I couldn't believe anything he had told me, that he only wanted to seduce me into defenselessness—and then what, what had he planned to do?

Ezra said, "Get away from her," and he stepped forward again.

Carey straightened his arm, his gun trained on Ezra's chest.

Ezra put his hands in the air—I surrender—but took another step closer.

"Put the gun down," I said, and Carey aimed the gun at me instead, at my face. I held my breath.

I took one step back at the same time Ezra took one step forward, and Carey pointed the gun back at him.

Ezra and I had a game we used to play when we were first together: How long could we conduct a conversation with improvised hand signals instead of speech? Would you like an apple? Yes, with some peanut butter, please. Maybe we should get another cat. I'm not ready for another cat. We should go to bed. I know, it's late, but read me another chapter, pretty please.

Ezra stepped forward, and I met his glance. The gun stayed on Ezra. Carey took a step back. The gun was on me. I stepped forward again. Ezra did, too. The gun was on him now, fixed on him. Ezra was looking at me, not Carey, blinking, one, two, three—

And that was when I lunged forward and shoved my right hand flat against Carey's sternum, once, hard, as hard as I could, up at an angle, my hand landing squarely over his heart. Carey stumbled back, his sneaker slipping on the slate, and he reached out to me, to grab hold of me, but he couldn't and took a second step back, except this time his foot had nowhere to go.

He made no sound when he fell, and there was no sound when he landed on the rocks, already a ghost, no sound at all.

5

EVEN NOW, ACROSS THE CONTINENT AND IN A DIF-
ferent country, I will occasionally follow a random
stranger. Not long ago there was a young woman driving
an old station wagon through a forest. It was very early,
the fir line coming into view at dawn. I pulled into a rest
stop when she did and only pretended to fill up my car
with gas. I watched her unstrap a toddler from the back
seat, lift him out, and set him on the ground. She knelt
to wipe his nose and retie his sneakers. I could see the
boy complain that now his sneakers were too tight, although it was possible he'd object to anything his mother
did, like making him get out of the warm car in the first
place, like driving all night. A little cloud of steam shot
out from the child's mouth in the cold dawn. I wanted to
roll down my window and tell him to pretend his breath
was dragon fire. Were they on the run? From what or
from whom? Unpaid bills, someone abusive, some other

misery—or maybe for good solid reasons, a reunion, a new chapter in a new place. The mother rebuckled her son into the car seat and pulled his scarf up over his nose. She removed the nozzle from her gas tank and slipped in behind the wheel. The station wagon pulled back out onto the highway. I let them go.

Of all the people I'd followed wherever I'd wandered, I found myself most melancholic when tracking mothers with young children. By now I knew what emotions I'd work through, the specific grief for a life not lived, and maybe this was what drove those of us who had engaged in the game with any kind of fidelity: the desire to track anyone we suspected might be very much like us but who occupied a shadow plane. Maybe this was why we kept playing long after we knew better, because we believed we would come to understand our choices, to accept our particular stories, to achieve the serenity of mind that eluded us. Maybe this in part was what sustained our addiction when we knew our chase would only yield deeper loss—heartbreak, alienation, death.

After the station wagon was out of sight, I returned to the canyon in my mind as I often did, and as always I began shivering when I thought about what happened. It was autumn now, one year and one season later. There was a before and an after in my life, there always would be: the fact that a man very well could have shot me or thrown me to my death did not change the fact that I had pushed him to his. I still expected to be held accountable, although that anxiety was beginning to lessen. Mostly what I worried about was whether the private penance I had charted in the end really mattered. Would it be enough? Would it ever quell my restlessness?

I DON'T REMEMBER HOW LONG AFTER CAREY PLUNGED into the ravine it took for Detective Martinez to come hurtling down the exterior stairs of the abandoned house, but it wasn't long at all. She found Ezra and I huddled together, Ezra clutching me, trying to turn me away from the edge of the terrace.

"I told you to wait for me," she barked at Ezra.

She wasn't in uniform, but she had her badge clipped to her sweats, her gun out. She glanced around.

"So he didn't show up after all," she said.

"He did," Ezra said.

"Oh," the detective said, and took a deep breath. "Oh." She knelt at the edge of the terrace and looked down.

"He had a gun," Ezra said.

"I told you to wait," she said quietly.

"I called her when I found the note," Ezra said to me.

"I pushed him," I said. "It was me. I—"

"Quiet," the detective said, and stood and walked the perimeter of the terrace, staring out toward the property wall, back at the house, once again down into the granite cleft of the canyon.

When she returned to our side, she said, "It was no one."

"No," I said, "I—"

"Listen to me, Rebecca," Detective Martinez said. "You were never here. Neither one of you was here. And this is what you're going to do. You're going to hike out the back way and take the long way down to your cars. Don't talk to anyone. Then drive home and wait for me. Got it?"

My hand had been pressed against his chest long enough to feel a single heartbeat. I pulled away from Ezra and had to look again: Carey's body was twisted, folded in half, his hoodie pulled up and bunched over his head.

"Go home," the detective said. "I'm going to deal with this. I will be there as soon as I can."

At my house, my teeth wouldn't stop chattering. I was in shock. Ezra wrapped me in a camp blanket. I noticed his hands were shaking, too, so I made him pull the blanket over his shoulders, as well. It was the warmest day of the year so far, yet we sat at the edge of my bed cloaked in wool, trying not to tremble.

Ezra explained that when he went to confront Detective Martinez about being a so-called tour guide, she told him she was no such thing, that the police officers who had suggested this were pulling a prank on her, or—a more dangerous possibility—were on to her secret investigation.

Ezra asked what or whom she was investigating, and this was when the detective started to get angry with him: Who do you think? And he said he assumed it was the police running the stranger game network, but the detective wouldn't say more. Ezra asked if it was Allagash, and Detective Martinez told him to stop guessing, but it was clear from the way her eyes widened that it was.

What she did admit was that she was increasingly concerned that no one had found Carey—and did Ezra know if I'd had any contact with him? He didn't think so. She said she thought Carey was dangerous, and she'd hoped I would lead her to him, at which point Ezra became very mad and accused the detective of using me despite obvious risks, and Detective Martinez was done talking to Ezra and told him to go away. Before she let him go, however, she told him to find out if Carey had reached out to me and to let her know if he had.

We waited three hours for Detective Martinez to come to my house. She made us speak to her out back. The sun showed no promise of setting, and we had to shield our eyes with our hands.

She said, "Here is the story. I was looking for Carey as a material witness in my investigation. I knew he was connected to the wrong people and didn't have a way out. I wanted to help and suspected he'd still be in the area, and then I had a lead, spotted him, and followed him into the park. He knew I was on his trail and ran. I didn't want to lose him, and I lost reception when I should have called for backup. He scrambled up the trail to the abandoned house and ran around back, and when I reached him there and was coming down the stairs, he aimed his gun at me. I had my weapon drawn. And then I guess he knew nothing was going to go well for him, and he turned around, and he jumped into the ravine. At which point I called emergency services. It's a terrible tragedy."

I started to say something, but the detective shushed me.

"That is the story," she said.

"Thank you," Ezra said.

"You were never there," Detective Martinez said to me. "That said, it would still be safer for you now to leave the city."

"I need some answers," I said.

"I'm trying to help you," Detective Martinez said.

"I'm not going anywhere unless—"

"Fine. Ask away."

I wanted to know if what Ezra had told me about their conversation was true, and she said that the day after Garcia was pushed, she felt a line had been crossed. The police had been allowing all manner of stalking to go on, and they were providing cover for thrill-seeking burglars, even after two people got shot when the police didn't offer the protection they were paid to provide. They were collecting a few hundred dollars here, a thousand there—not extraordinary sums, but it added up. Citywide they were raking in a lot of money. But now they were countenancing, maybe even facilitating cold-blooded murder. Detective Martinez wanted to collect the most damning evidence and make the best case to one of the good-guy prosecutors who might still be around, and so she lied to me and said I might be a suspect in Detective Allagash's investigation so I would need to find Carey, and in doing so lead her to him.

"I regret this now," Detective Martinez said.

She was angry at herself for missing Carey when he taped the note to my door; her stakeout had been frequent, but not constant. After all, she was working alone, and she couldn't cover me twenty-four hours a day. When Ezra showed up at her house, she realized he could help and act as the lookout, too, and that was why she sent him to check in on me. It sounded like Detective Martinez was operating as a lone wolf, and I said she might be in over her head taking on Allagash and whoever else was profiting from the stranger game, because if this was going on in our city, certainly it was going on in other cities. Who knew the scale? Who knew the myriad ways this game had been manifested and monetized elsewhere?

"Thanks for your concern," Detective Martinez said, "but I'll be fine." And she added, "It may not seem like it, Rebecca, but I've always been on your side."

I wanted to believe this but didn't know if I could.

I stared at the back of my right hand, then my palm—
my own hand was so disturbing to me, my own hand a
weapon. Later Ezra would insist that Carey wanted to
make it look like I was the one who had jumped into the
ravine, a noteless suicide, that either this was what he'd
been told he had to do or it was his own dark plan. It
was possible he only wanted to frighten me so I would
stop going around questioning the police, but then again,
maybe Ezra was right. We would never know.

"I'll deal with Allagash," Detective Martinez said, "but
you need to leave the city now, Rebecca, and you should
not come back."

"Ever?" Ezra asked.

The truth was that I wanted nothing more than to
drive as far away as I could, but I was so confused about
everything that had come to the surface, and my befud-
dlement probably came across as hesitancy or resistance.
The detective withdrew a folded page from her pocket
and showed it to us: Carey's note.

"If you come back, I'll change my story," she said.
"You were already at the abandoned house when I got
there. I saw you push him. Of course, you might be able
to plead self-defense, but then who is to say a jury will
believe that."

"You just said you were on my side," I said.

"I am," Detective Martinez said. "You don't want to
be in the city anymore, not given who else might come
looking for you."

I thought she might insist on escorting me out of town, but she left, and it was eerie how calm I became—Ezra, too. I had already packed that one bag earlier and didn't need much else. If I was going to leave, I needed to leave before it hit me that I didn't know where I would go. But first. First I took Ezra's hand and led him into my bedroom, to my bed, where I sat him down, sat next to him, and reached over to unbutton enough of his shirt for me to slide my hand in over his heart. He was nervous, this was obvious. How could I make him less anxious? How could I convey to him that while our history was written, our future was not? I lay back on the bed. He lay back, too. We were facing each other. I unbuttoned the rest of his shirt; he took off mine. I needed to be held, and I believe he did, too.

It was night by the time I said, "I need to go."

Ezra understood. He said, "Then you should go."

"I guess it's my turn to wander," I said.

AND THEN I DRIFTED. AT FIRST I DROVE EAST AND NORTH, each night a different town. Eventually I started staying a week in a place, then a month. I volunteered where I could. I found temporary work in old brick libraries. I walked dogs; I delivered food to the infirm. I headed farther north and crossed the border, and when I reached the opposite coast, I stopped.

Meanwhile, I was in contact with Ezra, daily texts, calls at night. He would ask me where I was, and I'd ask him what new novel he'd borrowed overnight from the bookstore where he was working again. I knew he was lonesome—I was, too—but I needed my isolation. Occasionally he ran into Detective Martinez, who asked after me; Ezra asked her in turn if she thought that I remained in any kind of danger as a witness to an unsolved crime, and the detective didn't think I was, not with Carey gone. Although she maintained it was best for me to stay away. Ezra also asked if she was getting anywhere with her probe, and she admitted she was not. She didn't say it to Ezra, but Ezra said it to me: the bad guys won. That said, Detective Martinez swore she wouldn't give up.

I thought about Carlos Garcia all the time, about how he wrote his essay with the naive belief that his example could make the world a better place. How rapidly and viciously he was misunderstood. How tragic he couldn't stop what he never meant to start. How unfair, how awful the cost. My inability to accept what had happened to him in part was what kept me out wandering, perhaps. Could I at least live according to his model and erase all alienation and achieve greater empathy?

After I decided not to follow the woman with the young son any farther through the forest that autumn morning, I returned home to the old cottage I'd been renting, and I avoided the known creaks in the floor as I made my way back to the bedroom, where Ezra was still asleep. After a year away, I had asked him to find a broker and put my house on the hill on the market, which he did, and it sold right away. He'd been living in my house and said he would rent an apartment, but I told him I had a better idea. I asked him if he would come to me.

In bed, he pulled me toward him, and moored me there, and I could tell he was half-awake but didn't open his eyes. Later he would tell me he wished I wouldn't slip out the way I did, that I wouldn't go on these drives, and I would point out that they were less and less frequent, which was true enough.

As far as I knew the stranger game continued to be played in our old city and everywhere else, and given its various iterations and corruptions, I could not imagine what form it now took or what kind of networks facilitated how many daily invasions of privacy. No matter its traction, however, no fad could last forever. It would fade and be forgotten, but then what would replace it? Something, of course, something likely darker, but what?

The world was a world of strangers, and all anyone wanted, I had decided, was to be seen and to be known, truly known. So perhaps the boldest strike you could make against the stranger game was to see and to know one person as completely as possible: How could you draw a line connecting you and this one great love? How could you make that line indelible?

When I turned to face Ezra, I could see his eyes were open, blinking at me apprehensively. I smiled until he smiled. Be with me now, I told him. Be with me.

★ ★ ★ ★ ★

ACKNOWLEDGMENTS

I am grateful to my friend and agent Gail Hochman for her guidance, enthusiasm, and wit, and to my editor Peter Joseph for the care and intelligence with which he has ushered this book to its readership. I feel very lucky to have Gail and Peter on my side, and to work with everyone at Brandt & Hochman, Hanover Square Press, and HarperCollins.

My thanks also to my friends and family who sustain me: Charlie Gadol, Donna Sherman, Lano Williams, Joe Boone, Michelle Latiolais, Michael MacLennan, Scott Belluz, Marisa Matarazzo, Jamie Sher, and my colleagues at Otis College of Art and Design.

My world has been so greatly enriched by Kent Doss. I cannot imagine having written this novel or any novel without Stephen Gutwillig in my life.

This book is dedicated to Chris Tweed-Kent, who immediately became someone I felt like I had known forever.

ONE PLACE. MANY STORIES

Bold, innovative and
empowering publishing.

FOLLOW US ON:

@HQStories